Little House in the Arctic

An adventure story...

To Cheryl —
Kathy Slamp

by Kathy Slamp, M.Ed.

ISBN 0-9713345-3-6

Printed in the United States of America
2004

Dedication

To...

my two brothers

who shared this adventure

with me...

Contents

To the Reader...

Little House in the Arctic is an adventure story told about five amazing years of my childhood. World War II had just been won, and the United States was moving into an era of prosperity. Before prosperity could have its full impact, the U.S. was once again thrown into another world conflict—the Korean War. Our family was caught in the crossfire of these global conditions when my parents moved us from our comfortable life in South Texas to a rugged and frontier life of Fairbanks, Alaska and the North.

Throughout many years of teaching school, I have told and re-told these adventures to hundreds of students. As the calendar moves farther and farther away from the 1940s and 1950s, these true stories of five captivating years seem more and more unbelievable and even more fascinating.

Little House in the Arctic is a story of adventure and romance written for my children, my children's children, and the hundreds of young people I have taught. Ordinary life is sometimes more intriguing than fiction as these stories of my childhood illustrate.

Chapter 1
A New Baby and a New Life

Jason and I were both born during World War II. He was born toward the beginning of the war, and I was born right smack dab in the middle. During the war all men in the United States between the ages of 21 and 36 were required by the Selective Service Act to register for military duty. This system required every male to register for military service by his eighteenth birthday, and during the war everyone had to serve unless he had an exemption.

There were only five military exemptions, and our Daddy qualified for one of them. He was a pastor, and that classified him as *4D*—an exemption from military service. Daddy's *4D* exemption meant that he was part of the ministry, but his exemption from full time duty didn't mean that Daddy had no official responsibilities as a result of the war. Often ministers had the job of delivering KIA (killed in action) or MIA (missing in action) telegrams. So, Daddy did his service to the country here on the home front by sometimes performing one of these difficult tasks.

Since we were little kids, we had no say so whatsoever about where we lived. Our parents lived in South Texas in San Antonio, so that was our life. I don't remember much about the final two or three years of the war, but my memories accelerate around the time the war was over, and that is when my story begins. The war might have been over in 1947, and the boys had been home for a couple years, but America was still feeling the effects of the war.

During the war, all Americans did their part to help the United States win. Many women were called "Rosie the Riveter" because they worked in airplane and Jeep and tank factories that built a lot of the machinery for war. Families were encouraged to plant what the government called "victory gardens." These were just private family vegetable gardens, but by growing their own fruit and vegetables, these families were helping the war by making large farm supplies available to our troops overseas.

One strategic element about the war effort that I do remember is rationing. Each individual—regardless of age—was issued ration cards. A ration card indicated how much that person could purchase of a certain item. Rationed items that were in short supply because of the war were things such as gasoline, sugar, nylon, cotton cloth, and tires. Even though we were just kids, Mama and Daddy were issued rations cards for Jason and me. Somehow, having my own ration cards made me think that I, too, was helping win the war. In World War II everyone wanted to lend a hand to do his or her part to win the "big one."

Despite the war, my early memories are wonderful ones. Living in San Antonio was great. I don't believe that Jason or I would have ever known there was a war except we heard so many people talk about it all the time. South Texas was the only life we knew, and Daddy and Mama made it fun. Mama stayed at home with us and took us to Breckenridge Park and the San Antonio Zoo where we enjoyed great, fun days together. Sometimes she took us to the Alamo, and afterwards we would walk along the famous San Antonio river walk and eat enchiladas, rice, and beans at our favorite Mexican food restaurant. Possibly, Jason understood the significance and historical importance of the Alamo, but for me as a four-year-old, the Alamo was just a fun place to go with Mama.

World War II Ration books and stamps – A varying number of stamps was needed for each rationed item.

UNITED STATES
RATION BOOKS

UNITED STATES
OF AMERICA

War Ration Book One

WARNING

1 Punishments ranging as high as *Ten Years' Imprisonment or $10,000 Fine, or Both,* may be imposed under United States Statutes for violations thereof arising out of infractions of Rationing Orders and Regulations.

2 This book must not be transferred. It must be held and used only by or on behalf of the person to whom it has been issued, and anyone presenting it thereby represents to the Office of Price Administration, an agency of the United States Government, that it is being so held and so used. For any misuse of this book it may be taken from the holder by the Office of Price Administration.

3 In the event either of the departure from the United States of the person to whom this book is issued, or his or her death, the book must be surrendered in accordance with the Regulations.

4 Any person finding a lost book must deliver it promptly to the nearest Ration Board.

OFFICE OF PRICE ADMINISTRATION

Nº 238028 -90

In the evenings Daddy and Mama often took us to a small little amusement park where we would sit on wooden horses and ride the merry-go-round. Or, we would ride the live ponies or circle around in little boats that floated on an imaginary river. Occasionally, we bought ice cream from the Good Humor Man. Milk and eggs were delivered to the door as we needed them. We seemed to have everything we needed or wanted. Life was great, and life was warm!

On Saturdays Mama took our white Sunday shoes to the shoeshine man downtown who polished them for church the next day. I never knew where Mama got that custom, and it always intrigued me. On Sundays after church we ate at a popular San Antonio restaurant where an organist played music on the Hammond organ while we ate. When we left the restaurant, we kids were always given a balloon on a stick to carry out into the warm South Texas sunshine. It was a wonderful life that as far as I was concerned at four years old would just continue forever and ever.

One day, though, Mama had a surprise. She and Daddy went shopping and returned with three brand new dresses. By this time, it was 1947; the war was over, and it was actually possible to purchase clothes in the store without having ration coupons. Jason and I thought it was unusual for Mama to buy *three* dresses at once since we couldn't remember when she had purchased even one. Mama tried on the dresses for all of us, and I remember thinking that my mother never looked prettier than she looked the day she modeled the three new dresses. The dresses weren't the biggest surprise. These were special dresses—maternity dresses. Mama was going to have a baby!

Jason and I had never thought about other brothers and sisters. We were just little kids; life was good as we knew it, and we thought we were a complete family. But now life was going to change—and change forever! What none of us knew, though, (including Daddy and Mama) was that the new baby was only one part of major changes that were in store for our family in 1947. These changes would affect all of our lives (including the unborn baby) forever.

Daddy pastored a very good church, and it was a large one for his denomination at that time. We lived in a comfortable parsonage with a pretty yard. Mama put a swing set in the backyard for us to play on, and she had also made us a little picnic table just our size. Daddy was well paid for post war America. He and Mama often got to travel together out of town to church conventions, and Daddy was well respected and admired as a maturing young pastor. Today, people would say that he was on a positive career track, but in 1947 people didn't talk like that.

A few months after the big announcement, but before the new baby was born, Daddy returned home one day with a big announcement of his own. This announcement was so big that we nearly forget the imminent arrival of a new brother or sister. This new announcement was that Daddy had been appointed by his denomination to move to Fairbanks, Alaska to pastor a small mission there.

Fairbanks is over 5,000 miles from San Antonio. It is a totally different climate with four time zones between them. I was too little to understand anything about Alaska and cold weather, but Jason understood. We had never even owned coats, and now we were moving to the coldest part of the North American continent. A lot of preparation had to be made, but with it, there was a lot of excitement.

One thing was certain, though, there would be no moving to Alaska until the new baby was born. And so we all waited. The baby was not due to be born until September so that meant that our move to Alaska would take place after the cold weather had already begun in Alaska. In the spring of 1947 Daddy resigned his church in San Antonio so they would have an opportunity to hire a new pastor right away. Over night, our family was without a place to live until the baby was born and we could move to Alaska. That would not be until early October.

Daddy and Mama approached this unsettled time with a sense of faith, optimism, and adventure. Daddy spent the time from spring until October traveling around the country talking to churches and civic groups about Alaska. These talks also helped the denomination raise money for the mission work he would be doing when we arrived in Alaska.

But we had to have housing. Jason and Mama and I just couldn't live on the streets or at the mercy of friends and neighbors—especially when Mama was pregnant. The first residence Daddy found for us to live was in a vacant Mexican seminary. His denomination maintained this seminary in San Antonio for Latin American students who came to South Texas to study theology. We lived in the seminary during the summer when there were no students, and it was a great place for Jason and me. The seminary was large enough to accommodate several dozen students, but Mama, Jason, and I were all alone there except for the times that Daddy was home from his money raising trips.

Several interesting events happened while we lived at the seminary. All four of us got the mumps. But we didn't get them at same time. Jason got them first, then two weeks later, I got them, and finally both Daddy and Mama got the mumps. Our family had the mumps for nearly two months straight. Mama also thought I should have my tonsils taken out before we moved, so I had a tonsillectomy while we lived at the seminary. I'll always remember that day. The smells at the hospital made Mama so sick that the doctor sent me home as soon as the surgery was over.

The Mexican seminary had a large, screened in porch that wrapped around the building, and Mama let Jason and me sleep out there some nights. We would lie there in the humid Texas nights on little cots, listening to crickets and watching fireflies flit by and looking at the evening stars. It was so hot and humid that all we needed for cover was one single sheet. All the while, Mama kept the long days filled with trips to the zoo and the park.

Mama had a favorite seafood restaurant downtown that she often took us after our excursions. One day at that restaurant Mama choked on a fishbone. Jason and I watched in horror as the restaurant owner rescued her from choking to death. Little did any of us understand how soon our life in South Texas would be gone forever and those sights and sounds of the South would be replaced with brand new sights and sounds of the North—sights and sounds and experiences that none of us could even imagine.

When early fall arrived, our family had a new dilemma. The seminary students began to return from Mexico and Central America, and it was no longer possible for us to stay at the seminary. Daddy was forced to find someplace else for us to live. Since our stay at this next place would be short—possibly one to two months—he looked for an inexpensive apartment. He found one all right. I remember that apartment as a rundown two-story building.

Our apartment was on the second floor. There was no air-conditioning in those days, and the end of summer 1947 was stifling as we waited the final days and weeks for the arrival of the new baby. We had always lived in a house in a neighborhood, so the apartment was exciting for Jason and me. It had a front balcony that faced the street. On stifling summer evenings Mama sat with us on the balcony with our new neighbors attempting to escape the hot apartment and enjoy what little breeze might be blowing.

One night as we sat on the balcony, there was a fight in an apartment below us. Shortly, the police came in their paddy wagon and carried away a man from the floor below. This was a brand new world to me. Our home had always been calm. I couldn't believe that people could scream and yell at one another so much that the police would need to come. I was wide-eyed, and Mama tried to shelter Jason and me from what was happening, but it was virtually impossible in our tiny little apartment.

After this big event, the rest of the summer seemed quite dull as the three of us waited for the new baby. It was at the apartment that Mama introduced us to the popular radio shows of that time: *Fibber McGee and Molly, Digger O'Dell, Amos and Andy, The Lone Ranger*, etc. That summer Mama was busy making preparations for our big adventure to Alaska as well as getting ready for a new baby.

One of the biggest preparations necessary for Daddy and Mama to make for our move was to buy our family a new car. During the war, Daddy—like most Americans at home—got by with whatever car was available. New cars were unheard of during World War II. Actually, Daddy was more fortunate than most people because gasoline was one of the biggest rationed items.

Since Daddy was a minister, though, and needed in the community, he was always able to get gasoline ration cards, but seldom tire ration cards. Many Americans during the war didn't even drive cars.

It was part of the war effort to conserve resources. People took the bus or walked. New tires were unheard of. Tires were rationed just like sugar, coffee, and other items. Daddy's old Mercury had broken down numerous times, and finally it caught on fire. There was no way that old car was going to Alaska.

The mission board told Daddy that if possible they wanted him to buy a brand new vehicle to drive to Seattle and then have it shipped to Fairbanks. It is a relatively easy task these days to buy a new car, and it's nearly impossible now to understand how difficult it was in 1947 for Daddy to purchase our family a new car. Today, there are car dealerships on every corner and television ads blare night and day about the deals they can offer consumers.

This wasn't the case in 1947. To begin with, Daddy had to put his name on a list even to qualify to buy a new car. Then, all he could do was wait for the automobile agencies to call him and let him know they had an available new car. Daddy didn't get to choose the color or the model or even the brand name. Things were different in the United States after the war. Even in 1947 when war had been over for two full years, it wasn't easy to buy a new car.

After weeks of waiting, Daddy returned to the apartment one day with good news. An automobile dealer had notified him that a new car was available for us to purchase to drive to Alaska. All four of us were so excited—it was almost unbelievable. A new car! What kind would it be? What color was it? When would we get it? We all bombarded Daddy with these questions nearly at the same time. The car we got wasn't a brand new model, but it was close. Our new car was a 1946 Hudson Commodore sedan. It was a surplus new car from 1946 that hadn't been sold, and so Daddy was given permission to buy it.

I'll never forget that car. It was the first time in my young life that I had ever smelled a new car, and regardless of how old you become, you will always remember that new car smell. You always recognize it. It's a wonderful smell. And it means something. In 1947 it meant that the war was over and that Americans could begin buying new merchandise again. For my entire life until then, everything new was needed for the war effort, but we now could actually purchase new merchandise. The economy was changing rapidly, and our family enjoyed the change.

Hudsons haven't been made since 1957, but in 1947 our new Hudson was a *BIG* deal. It was a beautiful dark blue with four doors, six cylinders, a divided front windshield, and wings of glass on each door to adjust the wind as we drove along.

The 1946 Hudson was called a "step-down" car. That's exactly what you did when you got into it, you stepped-down. The floor was three or four inches below the level of the door and this caused the car to ride sleek and low to the ground. The

Step down backseat – 1946 Hudson

step-down feature made the Hudson appear like an extension of the highway merely gliding above its surface. The doors closed together in the middle. This meant that the front and back doors opened in opposite directions. When both doors were open, you could see straight through the car.

The trunk was nearly as big as the engine in the front, and it was an important feature for our move because it had enough room to accommodate all our luggage when we finally left Texas. We had an over abundance of luggage, but the Hudson still had room to accommodate it all. It was a huge car, and the step-down feature made it possible for Jason and me to stand up on the floor in the back seat without hitting our heads on the roof. The new 1946 Hudson was a marvelous car, and we were all enormously proud of it.

1946 Hudson Commodore

While Daddy was applying to the automobile dealerships to purchase the new car, Mama was busy packing and getting our things ready for the trip. The mission board advised Daddy and Mama not to bring any furniture because it was too expensive to ship it so far. Instead of our own furniture, the board would provide our family with a furnished parsonage.

The only things they told Daddy we could bring were our clothes, personal items (such as dishes and bedding), his library books, and of course, supplies for the new baby. Mama spent hours and days sorting through all of our belongings, deciding what to ship and what to leave behind. Most of our possessions were simply left behind because it was just too expensive for the mission board to send them all the way to Alaska.

When Mama pared down to the barest of essentials, she and Daddy bought a big blue metal trunk to ship our family pictures and sentimental pieces in. That trunk was so neat! It was three feet long and two and a half feet tall. It had bright yellow bronze hinges and a big bronze padlock on the front. When you lifted the lid, inside there was a big divided tray that fit all the way across the top. Beneath the tray, the remainder of the trunk was available for storing sheets, blankets, and whatever else Mama needed to store.

I'll never forget that trunk as long as I live. After we got to Alaska and had a lot less furniture than we had been accustomed to, the trunk became a valuable piece of furniture. The trunk was our reading center. Before I ever learned to read for myself, Jason and I sat together on the blue trunk, and he read aloud to me. Everywhere our family ever moved after that the blue trunk went with us.

By summer's end, all our preparations for the big move were completed; we were set to go. All the preparations but one that is. We still didn't have the new baby! And so we all waited. And while we waited in the warmth of the South Texas sunshine, it was beginning to snow in Alaska, and the Arctic winter was settling in.

In the third week of September, the new baby arrived. He was a boy, and Mama and Daddy named him Samuel, but he was Sammy to us. Mama and Daddy were excited, not only because the baby was healthy, but also because his arrival meant that we could begin our big journey north.

Together in that old apartment house in San Antonio, Mama and Daddy made the final arrangements for our drive across the United States to Seattle, Washington. In Seattle, we would board a plane and fly to Fairbanks, Alaska. And while they were making their arrangements, we were all attempting to get comfortable with Sammy's arrival and his new permanent presence in our lives. When

Sammy was only two weeks old, Mama and Daddy packed our new blue Hudson with all the things necessary for the 3,300 mile drive across the continental United States, and we began our journey from Texas to Seattle. Mama and Daddy said their final Texas "good byes," and early one October morning we begin driving North and West.

None of us knew on that warm fall day how this trip would change our lives forever and how it would bring unbelievable adventure and lifelong memories to the five of us. As a four-year-old, there was no way I could grasp the extent of the changes that were beginning to take place in our lives. Daddy was just responding to what he felt he should do, Mama thought it was a great adventure, and Jason and I were too young to understand all the adventure that lay ahead. Little Sammy was brand new, totally dependent, and along for the ride of his new little life.

Chapter 2
The Long Long Trip North

On October 9, 1947, our family drove north from San Antonio, Texas and began our long journey to Alaska. It took us nearly two weeks to wind our way across the United States, saying our good byes to family and friends as we went. Daddy had left us home while he went out on his speaking and money raising engagements, but on our route to Seattle he had three additional services that we attended with him.

Little Sammy was only three weeks old when we left San Antonio, and all he did was sleep or cry. Jason and I, on the other hand, were wide-eyed at all the adventures and spectacles we encountered during our westward expedition. The early pioneers and wagon trains had nothing on us; we determined not to miss a thing.

On Thursday, October 9, we drove to Elk City, Oklahoma—611 miles from San Antonio. Elk City, a little city in Western Oklahoma, is certainly not a traditional tourist stop, but this wasn't a tourist trip. Mama and Daddy were both raised in Elk City; in fact, they had practically been raised together. Daddy had first noticed Mama when she was thirteen and he was sixteen. Although they didn't start dating until a few years after that, they married when Mama was nineteen and Daddy was twenty-two. Daddy and Mama went to the same high school and lived in the vicinity of Elk City all their lives. Consequently, there were many friends and family in Elk City for them to tell "good bye."

Daddy's father still lived in Elk City, and his sister lived a few miles away in West Texas on a ranch. Even though Mama's mother had moved to Oregon, Elk City was still full of her cousins, aunts and uncles, and classmates. We spent three days in Elk City showing off the new baby and telling everyone good by. Many of Mama and Daddy's family and friends thought they had literally lost their minds to move to Alaska. How in the world could they justify leaving the South and taking their little family so many thousand miles away? These people just didn't have the sense of adventure that Daddy and Mama had.

Mama and Daddy were undaunted by all these objections and forewarnings. Both of them were excited about our big adventure. After Daddy had spoken in the little church where he grew up and enlightened them about our mission, it was time to leave the family. On Monday, October 13, 1947, we headed west from Elk City toward Colorado.

The summer of 1946 Daddy had taken our family to California on a vacation, but *none* of us had ever been as far as the Pacific Northwest! Our first stop after Elk City was Trinidad, Colorado. Daddy only drove 384 miles that day, and Mama and the new baby were very tired. She kept the baby and me with her in a little hotel room while Daddy took Jason to another speaking engagement he had that night in Trinidad.

Little Sammy was adjusting pretty well to his new world, but his feeding regimen had to be altered. Mama's doctor advised her against nursing Sammy since the trip itself would be too hard for her after just having a new baby. Also—quite wisely—he advised her against formula or cow's milk for the baby. The doctor knew that in Alaska both infant formula and cow's milk would be too expensive on Daddy's meager salary. What the doctor suggested sounded strange for a new baby, but it worked, and it worked well. He suggested that from his first day that little Sammy be fed with diluted, condensed canned milk. Mama followed his suggestion, and Sammy thrived on this unusual newborn diet.

Tuesday, October 14, we continued our journey west. From Trinidad, Daddy drove across Monarch Pass in Western Colorado. Our destination was Twin Falls in Southern Idaho. Daddy had been invited by a friend to speak there about our Alaskan mission. In order to get to Southern Idaho Daddy had to drive across the vast open areas of Western Wyoming. Salt Lake City was Daddy's goal for that Tuesday, but we didn't make it as far as he expected. After 398 miles of driving, Daddy finally stopped for the night in Grand Junction, Colorado. Those were long days of driving in 1947 when the speed limit was between 45 and 50 mph. Mama and Daddy were incredibly brave to take on so much with two kids and a brand new baby.

In the late 1940s there was no such thing as the interstate freeway system that we take for granted today. Cars didn't run as fast or as well as they do today so daily progress was slower and tedious. There were no fast food restaurants; in fact, there were no chain restaurants. All the highways led right through the center of every single town, and we had to slow down for each and every stop light in even the smallest town.

Ultimately, we drove through the middle of every little village, town, and city all the way from San Antonio to Seattle. That really slowed our progress. As we drove through these towns, Daddy searched for a restaurant or fuel stop that looked clean and acceptable. Sometimes we were successful in finding a nice place to eat, but often we weren't. Sometimes the gasoline stations had clean restrooms, but more times than not, they didn't. We just had to take whatever came our way and be grateful.

And all the time, Mama was caring for a brand new baby. There were no disposable diapers or disposable baby bottles or anything even similar to that in the 40s. There were no infant carryalls or the convenient child care gadgets that mothers just accept as the norm today. Before we left San Antonio, Mama and Daddy purchased a little canvas infant bed for Sammy that they laid across the back seat, and Mama was forced to take care of the baby in the Hudson. Eventually, in some little nameless town, Daddy would stop at a laundromat, and Mama would wash and dry diapers, and then we would drive on.

As we drove toward Twin Falls on Wednesday, October 15, we had two memorable adventures. Far from most of civilization somewhere in the middle of Wyoming, Daddy and Mama saw it coming, but there was nothing they could do to avoid it. A large pheasant flew directly into Mama's half of the divided windshield. That bird just came from nowhere, and in an instant it shattered Mama's windshield. Obviously, nothing could be done about it, and so we continued on with a broken windshield on our brand new car. The glass was shattered but in tact. Daddy said the broken windshield would just have to wait until the car arrived in Fairbanks to be replaced. This turned out to be a good decision, because in the end, there were two broken windows on the Hudson when it arrived in Fairbanks.

Shortly after the pheasant incident, I was taking a nap next to Sammy's canvas crib when Mama shook me and woke me up. "Kathy," she said, "Wake up and look!" When I sat up and rubbed my eyes and began to look, my young eyes were filled with awe and wonder. Daddy was driving the Hudson extremely slow—about ten mph. The Hudson and the five of us inside it were lost in a sea of thousands of sheep. As far as I could see in all directions, there were sheep. In the late 1940s and before the Interstate highway system, many of the western states had open grazing. Several shepherds were herding their flocks across the landscape, and our car was trapped within the herd. It took Daddy nearly an hour to maneuver the Hudson through the flock and out again on the other side. What a memory for a little four-year-old girl.

As Daddy drove through this desolate part of the West, we began to see signs for a place called Little America. It sounded like a really special place. A rancher nearly froze to death in a blizzard in that remote region of Wyoming one winter. As a result of his bad experience, he decided that never again (if he could help it) would someone be stranded in this vast open land without shelter. So, in the 40s, he opened Little America. They advertised food, gasoline, rooms to rent, and stuffed mountain lions and sheep. We could hardly wait; this was going to be neat.

Exhausted and tired, we finally arrived at Little America, anticipating a pleasant stop. We were shocked! In 1947, Little America was nothing but a dirty wide spot in the road. They did have gasoline and some grimy restrooms, but there was no way that Daddy or Mama would consider renting one of their rooms. The food was bad and expensive, and there were only a couple mangy stuffed animals. Little America is now probably the biggest truck stop in America—and

San Antonio - Seattle
October 1947

October 9, 1947 - Depart San Antonio
Day 1:   Oct. 12 - To Elk City, Okla. - 611 miles
Day 5:   Oct. 13 - To Trinidad, Colo. - 384 miles
Day 6:   Oct. 14 - To Grand Junction, Colo. - 398 miles
Day 7:   Oct. 15 - To Twin Falls, Idaho - 544 miles
Day 8:   Oct. 16 - To Medford, Oregon - 684 miles
Day 12: Oct. 20 - To Longview, Wa. - 416 miles
Day 13: Oct. 21 - To Seattle, Wa. - 175 miles
Day 16: Oct. 24 - Depart for Fairbanks, Alaska at 7:00 AM
            via Pan American Talisman, Flight #901
            Arrive in Fairbanks at 2:55 P.M. (Alaskan time)

one of the cleanest and nicest. It is a large corporation with first class hotels in several western cities. In 1947, though, Little America was pretty sad. Pathetic, actually.

At last, we drove into Twin Falls, Idaho where Daddy was scheduled to speak for his friend. On Thursday morning, October 16, after our Alaska service in Twin Falls, Daddy headed the Hudson west toward Southern Oregon where we would say our good-byes to Gramma and Aunt Fran. Although Gramma loved Oklahoma with a passion, when Mama's step-dad died in 1945, Gramma moved to Medford, Oregon with her teenage son to be near Mama's sister. Medford was out of the way for us, but regardless, we absolutely had to see Gramma and Mama's brother and sister before we flew to Alaska. There were no extra funds for an additional night's stay in a hotel so Daddy just kept on driving and driving. After 684 long miles, we arrived at Gramma's house on October 16—the longest day's drive of the entire trip north.

Gramma was always an adventuresome, fun-loving individual, but she was as concerned about our going so far away from home as anyone. I remember her being more apprehensive about Sammy than anyone else had been. In 1947, Gramma had never flown so our flying gave her something else to fret about. Today, many families fly together and no one gives it a second thought. But in 1947, things were much different than they are today. Jet passenger planes were still in the future, and many people considered flying extremely dangerous and foolhardy.

Mama was crying when we left Medford. None of us knew what lay ahead or when we would be back in the states again with family. The majority of the public had never been on a plane, and there were few children who had flown. Daddy had flown several times, but none of us had ever flown, and Gramma certainly hadn't. Flying was an absolute unknown to her. As we prepared to leave Medford and head north to Seattle, Gramma had tears in her eyes as she held little Sammy and shook her head. She held him close and said to Daddy and Mama in a sad voice, "I'd sure hate to see this puny little baby floating down beneath a parachute!"

And so, after an Alaska service and our good-byes in Medford, we left Medford on Monday, October 20 driving north to Longview, Washington. Two of Mama's aunts lived there, and Mama wanted to tell them good-bye. Daddy spoke in a church in Longview before we left on October 21 and drove the final few miles north on Highway 99.

On October 21, 1947, after thirteen exciting days on the road and 3,238 miles from our home in San Antonio, our little family arrived in Seattle, Washington. Many months of preparation and waiting for the new baby were past, but we still weren't fully prepared to fly to Alaska. We had lived in Texas or Oklahoma for all of our life as a family, so we had *no* clothes for Arctic weather – *none*! And that included all five of us. In addition to purchasing new clothes, arrangements had to be finalized to drive the Hudson to the dock and have it loaded on a ship and shipped to Fairbanks.

Daddy's expense log of our 1947 trip to Seattle from San Antonio.

In Seattle, Mama and Daddy left the three of us on Queen Anne Hill with a babysitter while they shopped for winter clothes. And clothes they bought. Items that I had never seen or imagined. Wool coats and scarves, leggings, sweaters, long underwear, fur-lined gloves, wool socks, fur-lined hats, and even fur-lined boots. After shopping three days, we were literally loaded down with winter clothes. My new clothes were wonderful. I had a red snowsuit with leggings that had an elastic strap under each foot. My snowsuit had a matching hat and a muff. I was so proud. In South Texas I had hardly even worn a sweater, and now I had a snowsuit.

Daddy's new clothes made the most indelible impression on me. It was customary for Daddy to wear a dark suit and white shirt and tie, but now he had winter clothes like the rest of us. I had never even seen him wear a sweater or a raincoat. Now, he wore a long gray overcoat over his suit, black boots, fur-lined gloves, and a fur-lined hat. How different he looked to me. I thought he looked so distinguished and important in all his new outerwear.

On October 24, 1947, after the Hudson's radiator and engine block were drained for shipping, it was loaded onto the *Baranof*, a ship from the Alaska Steamship Company. The *Baranof* served both as a cargo ship and a luxury liner for passengers.

Daddy kept careful records of our trip north to Seattle. The mission board prepaid $272.64 to ship the car to Alaska—an astronomical figure in the economy of 1947. The total amount Daddy spent on gasoline for the entire trip was $52.88. Amazing! He spent $47.89 for three meals a day for five people, and the six nights that we stayed in hotels or motels cost $40.00 all together. It actually cost $131.87 more to ship the Hudson to Alaska than all of our traveling expenses for two solid weeks. This huge shipping expense for the Hudson was

Daddy and Mama's first taste of how expensive things were going to be in Alaska.

After all of the winterwear that Daddy and Mama could afford had been purchased, it was time to begin the final leg of our spectacular journey. On Friday, October 24, 1947, Daddy's friend picked up our family with our luggage and drove us to the airport for our flight to Fairbanks. Little Sammy flew free, but the other four tickets cost the mission board $448.50. The plane was a forty-seven-passenger Pan American World Airways propeller plane named the *Talisman*.

At 7:00 A.M. Daddy presented our Gate Pass to the agent, and we boarded the plane for Fairbanks. Mama and Daddy had paid for excess baggage, but they couldn't get Sammy's canvas car carrier on the plane so they just left it behind in Seattle. Our flight had only seven passengers—including the five of us. There were forty empty seats, but the plane still had to fly. It had a full manifest of passengers in Fairbanks waiting to return to Seattle on the *Talisman* two days later—October 26, 1947.

What an awesome experience it was to fly. I had no idea what to expect, but I found the whole flight extremely exciting and more than I had ever anticipated. I sat alone on this nearly empty plane and looked out the window at the landscape below. Below were mountains, rivers, islands, and oceans. My imagination transformed all this marvelous scenery into a giant amusement park with merry-go-rounds, ponies, and boat rides. I created my own imaginary world and loved every minute of it. The uniforms of the stewardesses, the airplane bathrooms, the in-flight meals, and the nifty seats that leaned back captivated my imagination.

Our plane had a scheduled refueling stop on Annette Island near Ketchikan before it completed its flight to Fairbanks. All of the cities in Southeast Alaska except Juneau are on islands, and in the 1940s none of them had a landing strip suitable for commercial planes. The land was just too rugged and the mountains too steep to build a landing strip. During World War II, though, the United States military

Airplane tickets - Oct. 24, 1947

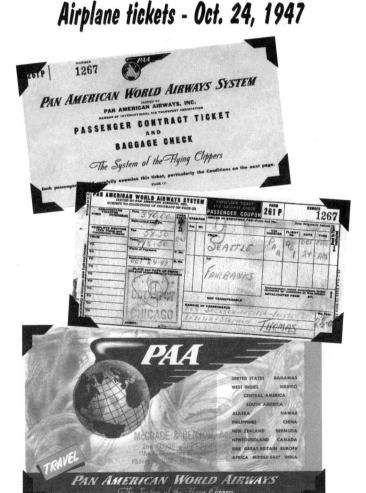

desperately needed a refueling spot in Southeast Alaska. They chose Annette Island—an island that had been settled by missionaries—to build a landing strip. Consequently, a large military post was soon established on Annette Island. Now that the war was over, military and commercial planes alike used the island as a landing and refueling spot.

Pan American Clipper

A severe snowstorm engulfed the area as the *Talisman* approached Annette Island and the pilot attempted a landing. Our pilot circled and re-circled the airport landing strip on Annette Island attempting to find a break in the storm. After several attempts at landing, the pilot made a judgment call that the storm was just too severe. He knew he had enough fuel to fly to Whitehorse, Yukon Territory for refueling. Thus, our refueling stop on Annette Island was aborted, and we flew on towards Whitehorse and then to Fairbanks. No one on that flight thought anything about the pilot's decision at that time. We thought the pilot was just playing it safe.

A little after 3:00 PM Alaska time October 24, 1947, and seven hours and two time zones after we departed from Seattle, flight No. 901 of the *Talisman* landed in Fairbanks, Alaska—over 5,000 miles and nearly two weeks journey from San Antonio, Texas. Sammy was exactly five weeks old the day we landed in Fairbanks. Winter had already arrived in the Northland; it was several degrees below zero, and there already were several inches of permanent winter snow on the ground.

In 1947 there were no jet ways, so our family stepped from the plane and walked down the portable stairway onto the tarmac. Instantly, we knew we were in another world. Snow was new to Jason and me. Once every ten years or so the Rio Grande Valley had a little snow that lasted a half-day. The previous winter we had had one of those freak South Texas snows, but nothing could have prepared us for the cold, long, northern winter. It was nearly six months after we landed before we even saw the ground again. I stood on the tarmac bundled up in my new red snowsuit shuffling my boots in the snow. What a cold wonderland we had ventured into.

Several people from Daddy's new mission were at the airport to meet us. Ours wasn't a mission as you might think of in Africa or India or China. There were a few Eskimos and Indians in Daddy's new congregation, but most of the people were either military or Civil Service employees who lived in Alaska. The rest of Daddy's small flock were people who had either homesteaded in Alaska or who had been there earlier in the military, loved the frontier, and moved back after the war to make Alaska their home.

After we collected our luggage, Daddy's new church members drove us to our little parsonage. This was my first introduction to our little house in the Arctic. Our trip to Alaska and our new home was almost over. But there were still two very significant events that happened that week—one scheduled, and one definitely unplanned. The scheduled event was the arrival of the Hudson via the Alaska

Railroad. The ship's journey from Seattle to Seward was nearly 2,000 miles and took seven days, so we arrived in Alaska before the car. When the *Baranof* docked in Seward, the car was unloaded and shipped by train the final 500 miles north to Fairbanks. A few days after we arrived in Fairbanks, the Hudson arrived.

We had grown so accustomed to being in the car that it didn't feel like we were all there without it. Daddy had the engine block and the radiator refilled, and then he had the car winterized. The window that the pheasant broke in Wyoming and a rear window that was shattered in the shipping were replaced.

After the Hudson was winterized and the broken windows were replaced, Daddy drove it back to our little house—totally renewed. Just as we had been compelled by the north to get new winter clothes, the Hudson, also, had to be readied for the winter. Now we felt complete, for we had all bonded with that car during our long journey north.

Two days after our family arrived in Alaska, an alarming chapter concluded our northern journey. This was the unscheduled event. The *Talisman* continued its flight north to Nome and then returned to Fairbanks. In Fairbanks, the flight crew changed. Eighteen passengers with its new flight crew boarded the *Talisman* in Fairbanks for its return flight to Seattle.

On this trip to Seattle from Fairbanks, the new crew was again scheduled to refuel at Annette Island. The same storm that had frustrated our pilot two days earlier had now picked up more intensity. The new pilot attempted a landing on Annette Island in the same storm that our pilot chose not to even try. He wasn't successful, though, and crashed into a mountain side killing everyone on board.

October 26, 1947 newspapers, including the *Seattle PI,* head-lined the Pan American crash. Among the passengers was the director of a Seattle church group and another family of five who also had a small baby. Many friends of Daddy's in the states confused this news and thought that our whole family had perished in the crash.

Years later, Daddy still had copies of telegrams and phone messages sent to Fairbanks and to his denominational headquarters with condolences for the loss of our family. It was an ironic ending to our amazing journey. Regardless of this plane crash, our family was safe in Alaska, and we were beginning a brand new exciting life.

No Sign of Life Reported from Plane Wreckage Found on Annette Mountain

The Salmon Packing Capital of the World

KETCHIKAN *Alaska* CHRONICLE

Vol. 100, No. 51   Ketchikan, Alaska, Friday, October 31, 1947   Price 10 cer

Climbing Parties En Route to Scene On Rugged Hillside

Several groups of climbers are pushing their way through the rugged wilderness to reach the scene of the wreckage of Pan American's missing DC-4 high on the peak of Tamgass mountain. The first parties are expected to reach the snow-covered wreckage early this afternoon.

While some parties were starting up the mountain from Tamgass lake, others were headed up the rugged mountainside from the beach. CAA and PAA personnel, Coast Guardsmen and civilians were included in the climbing parties.

Planes are circling the location of the wreckage to guide climbers to the scene and the Coast Guard cutter Citrus is standing by as base of operations to communicate with climbers, some of whom are equipped with walkie-talkies.

Latest reports this afternoon were that it may be night-fall before any of the parties would be able to return from the wreckage with any bodies they might find there.

The missing PAA DC-4 carrying 18 persons was sighted on a mountain visible from the Annette airfield at 7:45 this morning by a Coast Guard pilot, Chris Weitzel. He reported that the wreckage of the Clipper appeared to be burned.

The wreckage was at an elevation of about 3500 feet, approximately 200 feet from the snow-covered peak of the mountain which is sometimes called Tamgass mountain.

Weitzel said he saw the tail structure of the big clipper first. Circling, he saw what appeared to be additional wreckage and took movies with his observer, Tony La Monica, ARM first class. Four other planes they contacted verified that there was wreckage.

The tail structure was found on the north slope of the mountain, which indicates that Pilot Alf Monsen passed the lower end of Annette island and was circling back to the field to make an instrument landing in the foul weather which was prevailing at the time.

This appears to verify a report made yesterday by a native, George Williams, living on the beach of Annette island opposite Bold island, who said he heard a plane at about 1:30 Sunday and then a loud noise.

Chapter 3
Fairbanks — The Golden City

Life in Alaska today is similar to life in the lower forty-eight, but in the late 40s when our family moved to Fairbanks, there were many differences and contrasts. How the United States came to own Alaska in the first place is a colorful story that intrigued me as a little girl.

This remote, frozen wasteland was purchased from Russia soon after the American Civil War in 1867 during the presidency of Andrew Johnson. Before 1867, Alaska was a fur-trading outpost for the Russians. After Russia lost the Crimean War in the 1850s, this vast area became a liability to them. Russian tried everything imaginable to make Alaska profitable, including selling ice to San Francisco. During the 1860s, Russia finally decided to sell this property that they considered a frozen, worthless wasteland. In that era, stove top beaver hats were all the rage in the United States. So, in a large part, Alaska was purchased to provide beaver pelts for hats and lap robes for wealthy, stylish Americans of the 19th Century.

This real estate transaction that took place between Russia and the United States was the largest of all time. On a chilly October day

in 1867, on Castle Hill in the Russian capital of Sitka, Russian can-
ons fired a final signal out to sea. While the Russian flag (which had
flown in Alaska for 126 years) was lowered, the thirty-seven star
American flag was raised. In the time it takes to lower a flag, 17 of
North America's highest mountains, icy Arctic lakes, rivers filled
with salmon and trout, glaciers, snow, tundra, billions of dollars of
yet to be discovered gold and oil—literally millions of acres of
unexplored, virgin land—were transferred to the United States. The
total cost of Alaska was $7.2 million. This price equaled about two
and a half cents per acre. What a deal! But the American people
didn't think so.

Texas was the largest state in 1867, but the purchase of the
Territory of Alaska gave the United States a piece of real estate nearly
five times the size of Texas. History is unmistakably clear that the
purchase of Alaska was the biggest real estate coup of all time. But
in 1867, citizens of the United States thought this purchase was a big
joke and an absolute waste of money. President Andrew Johnson
was a very unpopular president anyway, and the American people
just laughed at him and his purchase. People referred to Alaska as
"Seward's Folly," "Johnson's Ice Box," "Icebergia," and other such
names of ridicule. For nearly thirty years, Alaska was a geographic
eyesore to the United States. Many people suggested that we get rid
of it—just dump it. All this public ridicule was soon to change,
however, and change forever.

In 1896, nearly thirty years after the purchase of Alaska, gold
was discovered in the Yukon. This set off a human stampede of epic
proportions. With the discovery of gold in the Arctic, hundreds and
thousands of Americans changed their tune about Alaska being worthless. The discovery of Alaskan gold began one of the biggest gold

rushes in world history. People flocked to Alaska and the Yukon Territory from all parts of the United States and the world. Skagway in Southeast Alaska became a boom town almost over night.

Many of these prospectors and adventure seekers were totally unprepared for the journey north or for the unbelievable environmental elements they encountered once they arrived in Alaska. Few of the 98ers (as the prospectors were called) actually struck it rich in gold, but a few who didn't discover gold, got rich through other schemes. The majority, however, didn't strike it rich in gold or make a bonanza through any other means.

When our family arrived in Alaska in the late 1940s, Fairbanks was still a "new town." The gold rush of the 1890s didn't reach the interior of Alaska until 1902 when gold was discovered on the Chena River near present day Fairbanks. This discovery was conveniently situated about sixteen miles from a small trading post that had been started one year earlier by a riverboat captain named E. T. Barnette. E. T. Barnette and his wife Isabelle were two extremely colorful individuals.

The Barnettes came to Alaska in 1897 with "Klondike fever" but never struck it rich. When Barnette realized that he probably wasn't going to strike gold, he decided to establish a trading post near the Tanana Crossing. Here, he planned to sell necessary supplies to other miners and prospectors—at inflated prices. Immediately after he made this decision, Barnette returned to California and purchased $20,000 worth of supplies for his new trading post. If he couldn't make it rich one way, he would make it another.

In April 1901, Barnette and his wife Isabelle purchased the little ship named *Arctic Boy* for $10,000. Their plans to use the ship to shuttle their supplies to his new city were dashed when the *Arctic Boy* struck a rock that tore the bottom out of the boat. Barnette was now desperate. He took out a $6,000 loan from Captain Adams of the *Lavelle Young* and in return agreed to pay Adams one-third of his profits from the trading post. Captain Adams agreed to transport Barnette and his wife and their $20,000 worth of supplies north on the *Lavelle Young*.

This little ship didn't reach Barnette's destination either. It kept getting stuck in shallow water, and Captain Adams blamed the Barnettes and kicked them off his boat. Not to be deterred by this minor setback, the determined couple simply set up their trading post at the spot where Adams kicked them off the boat— the spot where the Chena River and the Tanana River meet. They named their trading post "Barnette's Cache." This happenstance of history proved to be "Barnette's bonanza."

Meanwhile, an aimless prospector named Felix Pedro was wandering the area near Barnette's Cache. It was customary for Pedro to stop by Barnette's Cache and shoot the breeze and brag about his expeditions with ET and Isabelle. Many prospectors had the reputation of talking big, so no one paid much attention to Pedro's boasting. In their minds, this sickly little man from Italy was just one more luckless drifter.

On July 28, 1902, however, Pedro walked into the trading post and announced that he had "struck it." Somehow, Pedro convinced Barnette that he had indeed hit the mother lode—the bonanza. It was a bonanza all right—the big one! Between 1905 and 1906 alone, over fifteen million dollars of gold was taken from the hills and rivers around this new town of Fairbanks. Quickly, Barnette altered his plans to move the trading post. He would begin his town in this very spot—twelve miles from Pedro's big strike. It worked, and Fairbanks was begun.

Until the discovery of gold, the only people living in the area of Fairbanks were Athabascan Indians. Alaska had been their home for thousands of years. That's all Fairbanks was until 1902—just a small trading post on the Chena River in the Tanana Valley near an Indian village. Even its name was deceiving. Many people thought that the name Fairbanks had something to do with the river. There was nothing "fair" about Fairbanks—especially in the winter! It was bleak. Once gold was discovered near his trading post, Barnette convinced the U.S. judge to name the town after the U. S. Vice President, Charles Fairbanks. The Vice President was the judge's boss, and Barnette thought that naming this outpost after the Vice President would encourage his support of Fairbanks with federal funds.

Despite the terrible cold weather, Fairbanks grew rapidly after the discovery of gold. By 1903 Fairbanks had its own court, jail, post office, telephone and telegraph office, and a department store. This store began only as a trading post, but by the time our family arrived in 1947, the Northern Commercial Co. was the only really respectable place in Fairbanks to shop. By 1910—in only eight brief years—Barnette's tiny trading post at Fairbanks grew to over 3,500 residents. In addition, there were at least 6,000 miners working claims in the area.

In 1923 the Alaskan Railroad was constructed from Fairbanks in the north to Seward in the south. This railroad was an amazing engineering feat to build and maintain over such diverse land and wilderness areas with its many rivers and abundance of wildlife. It was famous for its long, high trestles and winding roadbeds. Through some of the mountain passes the train would slow to 10 mph. In these passes, passengers in the middle of the train could literally see the engine and the caboose at the same time. The train rapidly became the vital connecting link between the interior and the coast. The railroad played a vital role in the settlement of Alaska, and without the railroad, Alaska wouldn't be what it is today. Between the discovery of gold in the early 1900s and the arrival of the railroad in 1923, Fairbanks had become a city in its own right.

The pioneer spirit that our family experienced in 1947 was fueled in part by the presence of the early "sourdoughs" in the territory. Sourdough was a nickname for anyone who survived the gold rush or one winter in Alaska. The pioneers and prospectors had several definitions for a sourdough. Until you had spit in the Yukon River, or flown over the Arctic Circle, or spent one full winter in Alaska, you were considered a *Chichaca* (an Indian word for a newcomer or an outsider). When you had done any one or more of these things, you passed the unwritten Alaskan test of survival and were considered a sourdough.

When we arrived, many of these old sourdoughs were still in the Fairbanks vicinity living in their log cabins with the sod roofs. In the summer time, these sod roofs were a marvel by themselves. The old sourdoughs allowed raspberries and wild flowers of all sorts to grow right out of the roofs. They were a bearded, rugged bunch that told unbelievable stories of Arctic winters, gold mining camps, and the wild life that prevailed during the gold rush years.

People in Fairbanks said that these old men were "soured" on the country and didn't have enough "dough" to get out. In truth, the nickname came from the sourdough pancake starter that many of these men carried inside their shirts in order to keep the starter warm. This always gave them a food supply at their next camp. The prevailing atmosphere in the north was ruggedness, and these old men supplied a colorful backdrop for our growing little city.

Even though the main gold rush was over when we arrived in 1947, Fairbanks still was the home of several operating gold mines. Huge dredges still sifted through the gold laden waters of the Fairbanks area, and hydraulic drills still blasted away at the rock, permafrost, and terrain to continue the mining of gold.

These giant machines were built on-site and were immense in size. For example, each dredge had a bucketline of 84 buckets. Each bucket by itself was over six feet in diameter—big enough to hold four or five adults. The dredges of Alaska's interior are relics of a bygone era and reminders of a once booming industry that captivated the hearts of thousands of men and women. Like the mastodons of the Ice Age are permanently lodged in the Alaskan soil, so these dinosaurs of the Gold Rush era silently rest today at the locations where they last operated. (See Appendix No. 1, p. 216).

The dredges all had names, but they were commonly referred to by their number: Number One – Number 10. At one time there were at least ten of these giants operating in various locations near Fairbanks—places with forgotten names such as Fox, Livengood, Chatanika, Chicken Creek, Upper Clear Creek, Eldorado Creek,Dome Creek, and Sheep Creek. All of these dredges were built between 1927 and 1940. Several of these were still operating in theFairbanks vicinity in 1947.

A dredge literally floats in water. It isn't necessary to have a large pond or river in order for a dredge to function and produce gold; it can work in shallow water. The purpose of the dredge is to separate the gold from the silt, gravel, and debris of the river or pond.

The entire process including the dredges and hydraulic blasters is called placer mining. Ester Gold Mine outside of Fairbanks—the largest placer gold mine in the world at that time with the world's second largest dredge—was always a crowd stopper on tours that Daddy and Mama took visiting guests from the outside. A gold dredge and a gold mine are awesome to watch and difficult to comprehend until they are witnessed. Because of the permafrost conditions of the Arctic, and in order to mine year round, the miners developed what they called hydraulic drills. These were giant hoses that produced a tremendous amount of water pressure. Operators literally hosed down the frozen hillsides and surrounding areas where a dredge was located in order to continue processing more and more soil through the dredge.

Another thing that was unique to Fairbanks when we arrived in 1947 was its enormous military presence. At times there were more military personnel than civilians. But, it hadn't always been that way. Before World War II, there was only one military location in all of Alaska, but the war changed that forever. World War II transformed Alaska from a remote, worthless frozen wasteland with a few gold mines to a strategic military outpost. Maintaining the safety of Alaska was vital to the war effort.

Few people remember that the Japanese attacked Alaska as well as Hawaii. On June 3, 1942, Attu and Kiask Islands in the Aleutian chain were attacked and captured. The Japanese were not driven from the Islands until May 1943—a year and a half after Pearl Harbor. The Japanese occupied the Aleutians for nearly a year. They had every intention of island hopping north until they took the interior of Alaska. From there, the Japanese planned to proceed down the Southeast coast of Alaska until they reached the Northwest states of the lower forty-eight.

After Hawaii was bombed in December 1941, Alaska was fortified to the ultimate extent. Since the shortest route to Europe and
Asia is across the North Pole, Alaska became increasingly important
to the defense of the United States. All of the United States was more
vulnerable until Alaska was fortified. Consequently, military bases,
outposts, and landing strips were constructed in all areas of the territory as a fortification against the Japanese.

During the late 40s, the presence of the United States military
was abundant in Alaska, and it still is today. Ladd Air Force Base
(now Fort Wainwright) was a driving force in the economy and
atmosphere of Fairbanks when we arrived in 1947. There were soldiers and Air Force boys everywhere—at one time over 150,000 of
them in the territory.

Daddy's church was on Noble Street, the main road that led to
the Air Force base. Often G.I.s came by the parsonage and asked Daddy
or Mama for help. Daddy and Mama called these G.I.s *service boys.*
They were all as far from home and family as we were, but they were
much more lonely. Many of them showed up at Daddy's church on
Sunday just to see someone from home. Once or twice Mama even
found liquor inside the front door of the church that G.I.s had stashed
there to pick up later. The G.I.s must have always been surprised when
they returned to get their liquor because when Mama found it, she
brought it home and poured it down the drain.

Mama never failed to invite the G.I.s and single civil service
workers to our little house where she served them a home-cooked
meal. On Christmas and Thanksgiving she would cook a huge tur-
key and invite as many G.I.s and civil service employees as could
come to crowd into the little parsonage for a "touch of home."

Two or three of these young people became permanent members of our family. One of these young men was Harold (from Tennessee). For years, Mama and Daddy referred to Harold as their third son. I loved Harold. He had beautiful, wavy blonde hair and spoke with a romantic, slow Southern drawl that always captivated me. Harold lived with us for a while in our little house, and even after we left Alaska for good, he frequently returned to our home for holidays and special events.

Another G.I. named Brad arrived one winter from Illinois and told Mama and Daddy that as soon as his girl friend graduated from high school, she was flying to Alaska to marry him. Daddy and Mama didn't know what to think about this. But it happened. Sure enough, one day Sally arrived in Fairbanks with her wedding dress in her suitcase. Mama and Daddy treated Brad and Sally like their own kids. Daddy performed their wedding in our little church, and I was the flower girl. None of their family could come, so we became their family. For a few months they rented the little log cabin on the church compound. After that, they remained a permanent part of our family. Since everyone was in the same boat because we were all far away from family and old friends, the bonds made in Alaska were often made for a lifetime.

Homesteaders were another major component of Fairbanks in 1947. In 1898, and again in 1930, the United States extended the Homestead Act of 1862 to include Alaska. The Homestead Act permitted an individual to claim 160 acres of unoccupied public land. The homesteader was required to build a home, live in it, and till the soil. If all these things were accomplished within five years, the land belonged to the settler, free and clear. A homesteader who couldn't live on the land for the full five years was allowed to purchase the land for $1.25 per acre after living on it for only six months. This was the last free land that the United States Government made available to the American public.

Alaska was indeed our "Last Frontier!" After the gold rush had run its course, many more Americans came north for another reason—free land. What these homesteaders soon learned, though, was that the land was demanding. There might have been little or no cost in dollars, but these homesteaders paid a high price indeed for their Alaskan homesteads. Those who succeeded in homesteading added to the rugged temperament of the general public. Alaska had a "can do" atmosphere in 1947.

Alaska did not become a state until 1959 when it became the 49th state in the union. During the entire time our family lived in Alaska, we were only living in a United States Territory—not a state. We paid federal taxes just like everyone in the lower forty-eight. My parents, though, were never allowed to vote in any presidential or national elections during the whole time we lived there. It was taxation without representation.

Alaska had two nonvoting senators that Alaskans elected and sent to Washington D. C., but they had no voice. We had a territorial governor and territorial laws, and we were citizens of the United States, but we were not a state. Statehood was always a topic of heated debate during my childhood.

Alaska was a rugged territory made up of a conglomeration of Native Americans, old sourdoughs, miners, military and civil service personnel, homesteaders, and a few *Chichacas* like us. People either loathed the place, or they loved it. Because Mama and Daddy had such a spirit of adventure, our family loved it.

Chapter 4
Our New Life in the Little House

Our new house reflected the spirit of the pioneers. It was the original church building that was built by a small group of people who began the church in Fairbanks. Many of the men who worked on the building were service men hundreds of miles from home who just wanted something to do and a place to belong. People told us incredible stories about building the little church during the winter of 1936. They had to heat the nails on a potbellied stove in order to use them. If they didn't keep the nails heated, the extreme cold caused the nails to break in two when they were hammered into the wood.

By the early 40s, the congregation grew so much in size that they built a bigger church next door to the little chapel. When they built the new church, the original little chapel was converted into a parsonage. A hot water furnace was installed in the new church that heated both the house and the church next door. After the new furnace was installed, the potbellied stove was removed from the little house. Radiators surrounded the walls of the rooms of our little house, and during the cold, dry winters, they produced a lot of static electricity inside.

The house was very simple. It was a one-bedroom house that had a traditional Alaskan storm entrance. The storm entrance led to a small room that protruded from the front door and was followed by a second door. This construction allowed us to enter the little ante-room and then close the first door before actually entering the house. We called this part of the house the storm porch, and it kept the death-like Alaskan cold from invading the living area of the house. The front yard was full of birch trees, and there was a wooden sidewalk that led from the street to our front door.

In 1947 Alaskan houses had a very unique feature that no longer exists in Alaska. The early Alaskan pioneers endeavored to create every way possible to insulate their homes from the intense Alaskan winters. One method they used was to collect all the sawdust created from the building of the house itself. Then, they built "sawdust boxes" around the exterior of the house. These boxes were about three feet high and six inches wide.

The procedure was simple: These little lean-to arrangements were filled with sawdust after the house was built. They were then sealed at the top and painted like the rest of the house. This gave the house an additional degree of insulation. It sounds funny today to describe sawdust boxes, but we were accustomed to seeing them and expected all the houses to have them. Our little house had sawdust boxes around all of it except the lean-to porch on the side closest to the church.

Except for the storm porch, our little house was totally square. When you entered from the storm porch, you were immediately in a living room that was exactly half of the house. The back half of the house was divided into two rooms with a tiny bathroom inserted between them. The right backside of the house was the kitchen.

Until we moved into the little house in 1947, the kitchen had a fuel oil stove. As a housewarming gift, the church bought Mama a brand new electric stove with a cooking well. The cooking well was the latest modern gadget, and it was like a built in crock-pot. Many winter days when we returned home from school, we were greeted by the aroma of a huge batch of pinto beans that Mama was preparing in that cooking well. The kitchen had a small lean-to shed that extended from it almost like another storm porch. The other half of the house was Mama and Daddy's bedroom.

The living room was lined with knotty cedar panels, and the aroma of that paneling gave our little house a pungent cedar smell. Windows were evenly placed on each wall, and under each window stood a radiator. Their continual crackling and popping was a sound that we quickly adjusted to hearing night and day.

In the corner of the living room was a built-in cupboard, and behind it was a bullet hole through the paneling. The former pastor was an avid hunter, and he nearly killed one of the church leaders there one day. They were talking while the pastor was cleaning his gun; the gun accidentally fired and shot directly over his supervisor's head. The initial shot frightened the pastor, and he jerked and shot again. This second shot left a hole under a radiator nearby.

All windows in Alaska were double. There was an inside window and an outside storm window. These storm windows were heavy, and each spring Mama or Daddy took them all down so that we could get fresh air into the house. Without these extra windows, though, our house would have remained cold through the long, dark winters.

I thought our new home was a neat house, and I loved the smell of the cedar, and the bullet holes just gave it a little more mystique.

All the houses in Alaska in the 40s had full basements. That was a blessing for us. If it hadn't been for the basement, our family of five would have been unbearably crowded in our little house. In one corner of Daddy and Mama's bedroom, there was a hole in the floor with a trap door. A ladder led to the basement below.

The furniture in our little house was rustic, but I remember it with nostalgic, sweet memories. In addition to the built-in cupboard with the bullet hole behind it, the living room had a sofa and chairs that looked like they came from a hunting lodge. They had fold down wooden arms for setting coffee cups, books, etc. Beside the largest chair stood a floor lamp. There was a large dining room table with fold-down leaves and wicker-bottomed ladder chairs. The kitchen had a tiny little table in one corner where we ate breakfast, but Mama served all of the rest of our meals in the living room. Each night we folded down the leaves of the dining room table and set the table for dinner in the living room.

Mama and Daddy's bedroom even had a Singer treadle sewing machine. This machine was not electric, but was operated solely by human power. Mama had to pump up and down on the treadle with her feet while she sewed. Regardless of the primitive way of sewing, Mama used this old machine to make a lot of great clothes.

Treadle Singer

Someone in the church gave Mama and Daddy a crib for Sammy that they put in one corner of their bedroom. Two little beds were placed in the basement for Jason and me, and each night we climbed

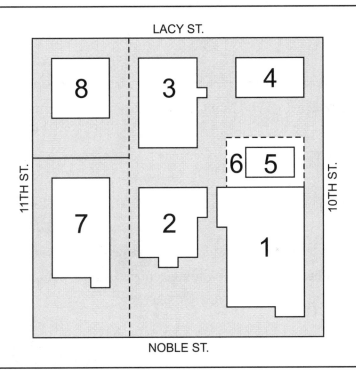

Layout of Mission Compound -1947

1 - Daddy's Church

2 - Our Little House

3 - The Rent House (contained the well)

4 - The Original Log Cabin

5 - Garage

6 - Church Extension - 1951

7 - Neighbors who were robbed

8 - Neighbors

down the ladder to go to bed. In the basement was also Mama's electric spin/wringer washing machine. She, too, had to climb down the ladder to the basement to do the laundry. It was certainly too cold to hang clothes outside so most of the time the entire house was full of folding wooden racks for drying laundry.

In 1936, the church had purchased two-thirds of a city block on the corner of 10th and Noble streets. The little house where we lived was constructed first, and the corner of the lot was left empty for the "big" church which was built a few years later. An original, authentic sourdough log cabin sat behind the new church on the corner. Between the cabin and the church was Daddy's garage. This log cabin was the home of the first pastor. When he moved into it, it had no running water or indoor plumbing. Behind the little parsonage was a small rent house. The church rented both the cabin and the house behind ours to military personnel who wanted a place to live off the base. Together, these four buildings created a little compound, and the entire area was ours to run and play in.

The rental house was built over the well that supplied water to all four buildings. Therefore, it was extremely important that the renter of that house understand the maintenance and care of the well. If the well was allowed to freeze, the pipes in all the buildings froze, and then all three houses and the church were without water. Freezing pipes was an enormous concern for anyone in Alaska in the 40s, but a freezing well was a catastrophe. Because of the well, the rent house held a strategic place in the church's little compound. Our first winter in Alaska we learned a vital lesson about the well. It must *never* be permitted to freeze.

In addition to paying his rent, whoever rented the little house behind the parsonage must agree to empty the hot water tank into the well once a week during the long winters. This actually kept the well from freezing. The well for the compound was 180 feet deep, and it was dug through three separate layers of permafrost. With the first signs of spring that year, the renter assumed he could halt his well-warming exercises.

As the earth began to thaw, the unsteady permafrost began to shift and stir. About the time the well began to thaw and the ground was shifting, the temperature dropped below freezing again. The well began to churn like an ice cream freezer, and it froze solid to the top. Daddy and a few of his friends tried for several days to thaw out the well, but to no avail. Finally, after three weeks and with the assistance of the city engineers, the well thawed out. That was the first of many lessons Daddy and Mama learned about our new Arctic home.

The lean-to that extended from the side of our house was precariously close to a larger lean-to that extended from the side of the church next door. (Daddy used this larger lean-to as his office and study). In the winter snow would pile up on the roofs of both buildings until it couldn't stay there any longer. Eventually, the snow from both lean-to's would slide off the two buildings, creating snow drifts as tall as eight to ten feet between our house and the church.

These small avalanches kept Daddy busy every winter clearing a path for us to walk between the little house and the church next door. All the streets around the mission compound were gravel or dirt; consequently, there were no curbs, and definitely no sidewalks. In the spring when the snow began to thaw, the area around our house (and everyone else's as well) was a huge quagmire of mud.

In addition to the four buildings that formed the church compound, there was one other house on our block. This house was next door, and compared to our little house, it was one of the nicest houses in town. The house next door was painted a bright white, had a much larger storm porch than ours, and was over twice the size of our little house. It looked like a mansion standing beside our little house on the church compound.

I wasn't one bit jealous of the people who lived in this house because I loved our little house. I was proud to tell my friends that I lived between the church on the corner of 10th and Noble and the big white house on the other corner of 11th and Noble. The people who lived there owned the big grocery store downtown, and they had no children. I thought they were rich.

One winter, though, an incident happened in the white house next door that made me especially glad that I lived in our little house rather than the big white house. While the five of us were peacefully sleeping next door, robbers broke into the neighbors' house. They tied up the neighbor's wife, and then drove him to the grocery store and took all his money. After the robbers got all the money from the grocery store, they brought our neighbor back to his big house, tied him up with his wife, and left them there. Somehow, the neighbors got free and called the police. The robbery was headlines of the *Fairbanks News Miner* the next day. We were shocked the next morning to discover that a major robbery had occurred right next door, and we were completely unaware.

I was never very afraid, though. I knew that we didn't have a lot of money that would make someone want to rob us. Before the robbery, Mama and Daddy had never locked the front door of the house or the church. After the robbery, Daddy continued to leave the front door of the church open in case someone needed sanctuary, but he began locking the front door of the little house.

Our family settled into the cramped life-style of our new little house next door to the church with a spirit of adventure. Mama and Daddy adjusted quickly to the pioneer atmosphere—they both seemed to thrive on it. They were happy, and so were we. The church next door to our little parsonage was just a few feet away, but it was still necessary to bundle up in our winter clothes to cross the yard to the church. The intense Arctic cold was merciless, and it demanded respect if you intended to survive.

Snow on the clothesline - 1947

That was the nature of the winter that had already begun when we arrived in October 1947, and winters in Fairbanks can be deceptive. I quickly learned that there are two kinds of cold. There is a dry cold, and there is a cold combined with wind and moisture. Fairbanks' cold was dry and still. Because of the dry stillness, the cold often fooled people causing those who did not respect it to have serious, permanent physical problems. It is common for the temperature to drop to over twenty below zero in late October and stay in that range and below until March. In Fairbanks there is seldom any wind. Several times during our life in Fairbanks, the temperature sank to over sixty below zero and just stayed there indefinitely.

Since the cold is dry and still, it often feels warmer than it really is. In other areas of Alaska, the weather is different, but Fairbanks' cold is uniquely still and severely bitter. One of the first lessons Mama and Daddy taught us was to always dress warmly to protect ourselves against the cold. In addition to all the winter clothes we had purchased in Seattle, we learned that it was necessary to layer the clothes. Mama always made us wear a wool scarf folded across our mouth. Without a wool scarf, it was possible for small particles of moisture in our mouth and nose to freeze as we inhaled. If this was allowed to continue for even a few minutes, our lungs could freeze. So, all of us were extremely careful not to expose our mouth and nose to the cold air.

Daddy and Mama had a friend who spent just one day on his homestead plowing snow off the road to his house with his mouth and nose exposed to the cold. He exerted himself so much that he frostbit his lungs. When lungs freeze, doctors say they look just like frozen lettuce, and they will not heal. Daddy's friend's lungs were so badly damaged because of this one day in the cold that he and his family eventually had to sell their homestead and move to Arizona. Their Alaskan dream was over because he had not respected the weather.

Old timers, homesteaders, and prospectors thought that the Fairbanks of 1947 was tame compared to the way it had been. Daddy and Mama, though, thought it was rugged. There were more bars than grocery stores. There were houses of prostitution up and down both sides of 4th Street near downtown. Saturday night downtown was pretty wild when the service boys and the sourdoughs all got drunk.

Prices were sky high—especially groceries and clothes. In Texas, we had been accustomed to having the milkman deliver eggs and milk and butter on our doorstep. Now, we adjusted to drinking powdered or diluted canned milk, and Mama had to restrict some of her baking because prices were just too high. When we lived in South Texas, we could pick citrus fruit from trees and have all the fresh produce we could ever want. Before we moved, none of us comprehended how long it would be before we would enjoy fresh fruits and vegetables again. After our first summer, Mama was able to store potatoes, carrots, and other root vegetables, but fresh garden lettuce, and tomatoes became a delicacy.

At Christmas the local market always gave our family a box of fresh Washington apples. These apples were packed in a wooden crate, and each apple was individually wrapped in blue tissue paper. These apples were a treat for all of us. On long, dark winter evenings, Mama would make popcorn, and we would eat apples and popcorn while Daddy read to us from the classics or fables.

When we finished with our apples, Mama taught us to lay the seeds out and recite this little jingle: *1) I love, 2) I love, 3) I love, I say, 4) I love with all my heart, 5) I cast away. 6) He loves, 7) She loves, 8) They both love. 9) He comes, 10) He tarries, 11) He courts, and 12) He marries. 13) Wishes, 14) Kisses, and All the rest are little witches.* The number of seeds left after all of this was supposed to be the number of children we would have someday. What fun!

After we finished the apples, Mama always kept the crates. They became chairs for us kids when Mama fixed meals for the service boys. This once a year supply of apples was all the fresh fruit we would see each winter unless someone came from the states and brought us fruit in their suitcase. Milk and bread and meat were four and five times more expensive than in San Antonio. Mama was creative, though, and learned to make bread and dinner rolls. She made the best cinnamon rolls in the whole wide world—complete with raisins. Mama learned to cook with powdered milk and canned vegetables and fruit, and we learned to enjoy it.

Once a year Mama ordered all our clothes for the entire year from the Sears and Roebuck catalogue. It was an exciting day when the Sears order arrived. There would be new clothes—pajamas, pants, shirts, gloves, socks, coats, etc. for each of us. Sears didn't make shoes narrow enough for my foot so Mama's sister in Oregon always purchased my shoes for me. If I was really lucky, I got to go down to the Northern Commercial Co., have my foot measured and X-rayed through the old fashioned machine, and then purchase store-bought shoes.

Occasionally, it was necessary to buy something other than my shoes at the Northern Commercial Co., but we couldn't afford that often on Daddy's salary. Luckily, Mama was a good seamstress and a pretty good sketch artist as well. When she found a dress at NCC that she wanted to make for herself or me, she sketched it, came home and cut a pattern out of newspaper, and then made the dress on the Singer. This way she made most of her clothes and mine, and they looked store-bought.

One year Mama got especially ambitious and decided to make each one of us kids an authentic Eskimo parka. What a project she undertook. She learned quickly that sewing with fur is entirely different than sewing with fabric. Once Mama set her mind to something, though, she got it done. And she always did it well. By asking around among her friends, Mama was able to acquire a couple old worn out fur coats that people were willing to give away. She disassembled these coats, laid the fur out, and cut out all the bad and worn spots.

Mama experimented with scissors and a knife until she finally discovered that a razor blade was the best tool to cut fur. She also learned that when sewing with fur you can cover a multitude of flaws as you piece the fur together. The one thing she needed to do was make certain that the nap of the fur all laid in the same direction. After Mama finished the main part of the parkas, she purchased some fox tails for the fur fringes around the hood and cuffs. Our parkas were works of art. Even the Eskimos were impressed with Mama's expertise with fur, and Jason, Sammy, and I looked like three little Eskimos.

Life was entirely different in Alaska than South Texas. Summer trips to the zoo or the amusement park were replaced with sledding expeditions and the Winter Carnival. The ice cream cones that Mama bought Jason and me on our way home from the zoo, were replaced by icicles. Icicles were plentiful in Alaska; we could just grab one from a building anywhere in town, and we had instant refreshment. Some of these icicles could be six to eight feet long, but we usually chose a baby icicle about eight to ten inches long for our winter refreshment.

We settled comfortably into our new little house and our new life. People at Daddy's church loved him and Mama, and they thought the three of us were pretty terrific, too. Our new life in the little house in Alaska suited us all, and all five of us thrived in the Arctic cold.

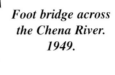

PHOTO ALBUM

*Foot bridge across
the Chena River.
1949.*

Raspberries on sourdough cabin - 1948

*Dredge at Ester
Gold Mine near
Fairbanks - 1949.*

Hydraulic hose blasting the permafrost.

The little house with wooden sidewalk - 1948.

The tightrope walker - 1948

The three of us in our parkas - 1950

Fairbanks' only school in 1947 - picture taken summer 1995
The ice skating rink was the left playground.

Holding back sled dogs before the race - 1948

Eskimos in gingham parkas at the Winter Carnival - 1948

Dogsled races on the Chena River - 1948

Eskimo woman jumping the blanket toss at the Winter Carnival - 1948

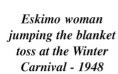

*Daddy and the three of
us in a grave - 1951*

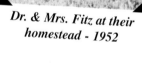

*Dr. & Mrs. Fitz at their
homestead - 1952*

A sod roof sourdough's cabin - 1948

Model of pioneer cabin - 1995

*A native
Alaskan
fishwheel
- 1949*

*A fishwheel
closeup - picture
taken 1995*

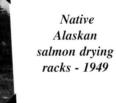

*Native
Alaskan
salmon drying
racks - 1949*

*A Wilderness
Cache near Mt.
McKinley - 1948*

Horseshoe Lake and Mt. McKinley (Denali) - 1949

Mt. McKinley Park Hotel - 1949 (later burned and not rebuilt)

Daddy in all his winter wear at Horseshoe Lake - 1949

Alaska Railroad winding through the mountains - 1995

The Anchorage hospital - 1949 (the best in the territory)

The Hudson between Fairbanks and Anchorage - 1949

Camping in the Matanuska Valley - 1949

Alaskan Fireweed - 1950

*A mastadon tusk
like the one we dug
up behind the
church - 1951*

*182nd Airborne
parachute drop
from Ft. Bragg,
NC - 1950*

The Alaska Highway - 1950

Alaskan Highway frozen waterfall

Crossing the U.S/ Canadian border - 1950

The Ford "woody" on the Alaska Highway - 1950

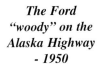

One-lane plowed highway - 1950

Whitehorse, Yukon Territory - February 1950

The Fairbanks winter fire of 1950 - over 50 degrees below zero.

Downtown smoldered for days, creating an ice cavern.

The Baranof in the Seward dock with the mountains and Resurrection Bay in the background - 1952

Daddy and I on the prom-enade deck of the Baranof - 1952

A passing ship in the Gulf of Alaska - 1952

Portage Glacier

The Baranof at dock in Seward - 1952

*Greek Orthodox Church
- Juneau 1952*

*St. Michael's
Russian Orthodox
Cathredral,
Sitka - 1952
This cathredral
built by the
Russians burned
after our visit.*

The five of us fifty years after our Alaskan experience.

Chapter 5
We Settle In. . .

Once our family moved into the little house next door to the church, we began to develop the same patterns that families follow everywhere. The first week we were in Fairbanks Mama and Daddy enrolled Jason in school. In 1947, there were only two schools in the entire Fairbanks area. One school was the public school two blocks from our house, and the other was a public school on Ladd Air Force Base. The school on the base was only for children of military personnel, so Jason was enrolled in the school two blocks from home.

Jason's new school was a large three-story building that held all the grades from kindergarten through high school. This building had everything inside. It had a gym and an auditorium, but no cafeteria. Kids either brought their lunches or went home for lunch. The high school was on the top floor with all the other grades on the other two floors. The local school board had been extremely wise when they built only one building because it was so expensive to heat a building. Having just one building saved the city a lot of money.

The school was modern for 1947. It was similar to Jason's school in San Antonio—with one big exception. Jason's new school had a large playground in front of the building. Except for early fall and late spring, though, it wasn't used for recess. When the weather dropped to subzero temperatures, a small two-by-four rail was placed around the perimeter of the playground. The playground was then flooded, and for the rest of the winter, our playground became the town's public ice skating rink.

On one side of the skating rink was the ice skating house. This was a simple little wooden building with no insulation or locks on the door. There were benches around the inside walls of the ice skating house, and there was a potbellied stove in the middle. An anonymous person kept a large fire burning in the stove all day long.

Jason and I would carry our skates over our shoulders to the ice skating house, take off our boots, and then with quivering, cold fingers, lace and tie our skates. Even when the fire was blasting hot, the ice skating house was always cold. We only had a few minutes that we could endure the unbelievable cold before our teeth were chattering and our fingers were getting stiff.

Once our skates were securely on, we skated on the playground with other kids. It was such fun to play crack-the-whip, Flying Dutchman, and other ice games. We never skated too long because of the cold, and when we were ready to go home, we had to repeat the process in the cold ice-skating house to get our boots back on. Whenever the weather warmed up to 20 below zero or warmer, Mama let us go skating.

Even when it was below zero, parents let their children go outside to play if they were properly bundled. We seldom went outside during school time, though. Too much class time was wasted changing clothes. What really made the school different from the Texas schools was the cloakroom. Every single classroom in the elementary grades had its own cloakroom; the high school kids had lockers. The cloakroom was the first and last place kids went every day. Each student had his or her own slot in the cloakroom to put away boots, parkas, snow pants, mittens, etc. Today, even grade school kids have lockers, but we had a cloakroom. And we needed it.

Even though Jason and I only walked a short distance to school, we wore several layers of clothing. When I was finally old enough to go to school, I dressed for school like anyone would today. I wore a dress, a tee shirt underneath, and socks and shoes. That was just the beginning. Before I left the house during the winter, Mama made sure that I had on at least three layers of clothing. First, I put on a sweater and long woolen tights under my dress. These were followed by a lightweight jacket and snow pants, called leggings.

Once all these clothes were on, I pulled a heavy pair of wool socks over my shoes and tucked my feet and the bottoms of my leggings into my fur-lined boots. Mama then wrapped a wool scarf across my mouth and nose and tied it at the back of my head. Before I put on my parka, I put on a pair of wool gloves and checked to see that my boots were zipped up tightly. The last thing I put on was my fur parka and my mittens. At last, I was ready to walk two blocks to school. This process was repeated at the end of the day for our walk back home.

Jason was always an excellent student and even though the Alaska schools were far ahead of the Texas schools, our three-week trip to Alaska had not set him back in the least. He loved school and fit into the new schedule well. I was so envious of his getting to wear all his new winter clothes every single day just to walk two blocks to school. I could hardly wait for school myself, but for now I had one more year to spend at home with Mama and Sammy.

Part of the parsonage furniture was an old upright cabinet radio that we listened to regularly in the evenings. I liked a kids' program called *The Cinnamon Bear*, but Jason wanted to read great books about history. Mama and Daddy agreed with both of us, though, that *Sgt. Preston and the Royal Canadian Mounted Police* had to be our family's favorite radio program.

Each week we listened spellbound to one more amazing winter adventure of Sgt. Preston and his dog King. We thrilled to the all-too-real stories as Sgt. Preston and King rescued people from Arctic blizzards or from the attack of a pack of wolves or some other such adventure in the wilderness of the Yukon Territory The Lone Ranger and Tonto had also made their way onto Alaskan radio. After hearing these programs just a few times, Jason and I could both recite the introduction to either Sgt. Preston or the Lone Ranger.

The highlight of the week for Jason and me was our Saturday morning trip to the library. Each Saturday the library story lady read to us. While I sat in the circle and listened to amazing stories of adventure and imagination, Jason looked for books to check out and read. Many of these books he later read to me sitting on the blue trunk in Mama and Daddy's bedroom.

One of our most memorable events of that first winter happened when Jason was reading to me while we sat on the trunk in the corner of Mama and Daddy's bedroom. Sammy's crib was in the corner of their bedroom, but we didn't have either the money or the space for a baby's changing table. All Mama had to use to take care of the baby was hers and Daddy's bed.

One day when Sammy was a few months old, Mama was changing his diaper on the side of the bed closest to the basement trapdoor.

The radio was playing, and little Sammy was bouncing up and down to the music. Jason and I were on the opposite side of the room sitting on the trunk reading. Just as Mama put Sammy down to change him, there was a knock at the door. Mother turned to Jason and said, "Watch the baby while I answer the door."

Jason was watching Sammy just like Mama said, but before he could run the few feet from the trunk to Sammy's side, Sammy bounced himself off the bed. I'll always remember seeing Jason dash toward Sammy as he bounced off the bed and onto the floor. Jason reached for Sammy's foot at the instant he made his second bounce over the edge of the hole in the floor and into the basement below.

When little Sammy hit the floor by the bed, Mama heard the thud and came running into the bedroom. Quicker than a flash, Mama scurried down the ladder to try to catch Sammy before he hit the concrete basement floor. Little Sammy's life was spared when he hit the final wooden step of the ladder before he bounced to the cement floor. Sammy was shaken, but Mama was upset. Unbelievably, Sammy wasn't permanently injured, but Mama wasn't going to take any more chances with our lives.

That very day Daddy and Mama called a carpenter to build a rail with a gate around the trap door opening to our basement room. After Sammy's accident and his near fatal fall, Mama was determined that there would be no more ladder to the basement. And so, a real staircase was built downstairs. No longer would there be an opportunity for any of us to fall through the hole in the floor of Mama and Daddy's bedroom to the concrete basement floor below.

Now that there were real stairs to our basement world, Mama worked hard to transform it into a combination playroom and bedroom for Jason and me. The basement was divided into equal sides. One side Mama converted into a kids' paradise for us, and the other side was her laundry room. Jason had a bed on one side, and I had one on the other. Jason's model train was in the basement as well as my dollhouse, dolls, and toys. There were books and games in our basement bedroom to keep us busy during the long, dark winters. Mama even hung a swing from the basement ceiling so that I would have a place to swing. Our basement world was magnificent. Neither Jason nor I noticed or objected to the fact that our bedroom also was adjacent to Mama's laundry and drying room. We thought this was the way everyone lived. It was normal for us, and Jason and I thought nothing of it.

Many times daily Mama walked through our room to the laundry room to take care of our family's laundry needs. Kids today wouldn't even recognize Mama's washing machine, but Jason and I were in awe of this modern wonder. This modern appliance was a tub that stood on three legs and had two compart-

Spin-dry washer

ments side by side. One side consisted of a large tub with a hose that pumped in water, and it functioned very much like today's washing machines. The other container was beside the large tub, and it was called the spin dry wringer.

In Texas, Mama hand fed each piece of clothing through a wringer, but not with this modern device. She took the wet clothes from the washing tub and then put them directly into the spinner.

When she pushed a button, the clothes spun around and around so fast that they were unrecognizable when she took them out. After the spinner finished spinning, the clothes looked like flat pieces of wet fabric. Mama had to pull the clothes apart before she could hang them up to dry. Dryers were not available to most people in 1947—especially in Alaska—so after the spin dry process, Mama hung clothes and diapers, etc., on lines and racks strung around our basement bedroom.

Our first winter in Alaska was an exciting adventure for all of us. Little Sammy was new to our family, and while we watched him grow and learn, we also learned about this amazing new world in which we lived. Getting adjusted to all the new clothes we were forced to wear was a big thing by itself, but cars, too, had to be babied in Alaska.

The first couple of winters were pretty primitive when it came to maintaining a car that ran. Each night Daddy put the Hudson into a little shed type garage behind the log cabin on the church compound. Next, he hung a 100-Watt light bulb over the battery and plugged the battery into a battery charger. Underneath the oil pan, he placed a one-burner electric hotplate. If he was lucky, the car could be coaxed into starting the next morning.

On extremely cold days, none of these precautions helped. On days exceeding twenty below zero, Daddy simply took the battery out of the car, brought it into the house, and wrapped it in a blanket to keep it warm overnight. The battery sat all night long on the kitchen table snugly wrapped in a blanket like another baby.

Our second winter in Alaska, Daddy purchased a head bolt heater. The heater eliminated Daddy's need for light bulbs and hot plates to keep the car's block warm. The head bolt heater was a little electric heater that kept the coil slightly warm during the long cold nights or days. At night Daddy just attached the heater to the car and plugged it into an electric outlet in the parking garage.

Regardless of the degree of cold or how much the Hudson had to be encouraged, that car never failed to start when Daddy had it plugged in properly to the head bolt heater. The head bolt heater certainly made it easier on Daddy than it had been the previous year when he had so much to do each night just to be certain that the car would start the next day. Head bolt heaters have been improved, but they are still used today in extremely cold weather.

Driving in the Arctic Alaska winters was totally different than driving in Texas. Antifreeze had to always be kept full and checked. Driving with low antifreeze would be like driving today with a fuel indicator light that showed an empty gas tank. Engine oil and axle grease for the wheels were both deliberately kept as thin as possible. Failure to keep your car in proper running order could be fatal. It was possible to freeze to death or suffer serious frostbite in a matter of minutes if proper precautions weren't taken.

Because the winters began early and lasted for months, it was possible to drive *on* the river. Fairbanks is situated on the Tanana and Yukon Rivers with the Chena River running through town. Some parts of the Yukon and Tanana were too deep to freeze enough to drive on, but the Chena River was always drivable in the winter. Driving on the river was so much fun. Daddy would just drive down the bank and *onto* the river. Actually, a lot of things happened *on* the Alaskan rivers in those days.

Our first winter in Fairbanks, we were introduced to the Winter Carnival. This carnival still occurs yearly in March, but it is no longer held on the river. So many chemicals have been dumped in the river that it no longer freezes like it did in the 1940s, but when we were kids this event occurred completely *on* the river. The Winter Carnival was a combination cultural, civic, and athletic event attended by everyone in town and the surrounding areas. The biggest attraction of the carnival was the dogsled races. Our family would walk up and down on the river examining all the various dogsled teams of huskies and malamutes waiting their turn to run.

Dog teams are paired two by two with a powerful lead dog in front with as many as fifteen dogs per team. The sled dogs are so eager to run that they sometimes have to be held back by trainers to keep them from running too soon. The dogs pull a traditional Alaskan dog sled with a musher running behind or gliding on the back sled runners. The driver whips and mushes the dogs forward across the ice as they race. The dogs bark and roar, and the driver mushes while the crowds cheer for their favorite team. What an exciting time the dog sled races were for our family.

The Eskimos and Indians didn't in anyway resemble the people in the pictures of the library books Jason read to me. In these books Eskimos wore fur parkas with big fur fringed hoods. When we arrived in Fairbanks, we couldn't understand how the parkas that we saw on real Eskimos kept them warm. They had the fur fringed hoods that we saw in the pictures, but the parkas of these Eskimos and Indians looked totally different than those in the books. Later, we understood what made the parkas different.

The early pioneers, prospectors, and miners who came to Alaska brought with them the colorful, gingham cloth that everyone used in the states. The Eskimos and Indians loved these brightly colored fabrics, so they simply altered their traditional wear to highlight the colorful gingham. The soft, warm fur that we thought was so beautiful and rare was commonplace for them. Consequently, the Eskimos reversed their parkas. They sewed the fur on the inside of the parka against their skin to keep them insulated and warm while they wore the colored cotton and gingham on the outside for show.

There were many native cultural events that took place on the river at the Winter Carnival. All together these cultural events shaped the traditional Eskimo Olympics in which the Eskimos performed many of their native Alaskan village games for the crowds. These games seemed unusual and peculiar to us. There were games such as ear pull, one and two foot high kick, knuckle hop, drop the bomb, 4-man carry, and the Eskimo yo-yo.

Jason and I loved the Eskimo yo-yo. The yo-yo consisted of two balanced sealskin balls that the operator spun in opposite directions on pieces of twine. After much practice, I mastered the Eskimo yo-yo and was proud of my cross-cultural skill. Everyone's favorite event at the Winter Carnival, though, was the blanket toss. We certainly had never seen anything like a blanket toss in Texas.

The blanket was made of a large round piece of whale or seal hide about 15 feet in diameter. It was held taunt around its perimeter by 15 to 18 Eskimos standing shoulder to shoulder. As they held this whale or seal skin as tightly and as taunt as possible, an Eskimo stood in the middle of this skin. Once the jumper was in place, the Eskimos holding the blanket began to move the blanket up and down together in one joint motion.

Simultaneously, as the Eskimos moved the blanket up and down, the jumper began to jump. The joint movements between the blanket holders and the jumper made it possible for the jumper to jump higher and higher into the air. As a little girl I would strain and strain my neck as I looked upward—sometimes beyond the tops of the telephone poles. Wow! What a sight. Jason and I were awe-stricken.

Twenty-first century kids are familiar with the blanket toss—they call it a trampoline. But in 1947, we had never seen anything like the blanket toss at all, and we were amazed at the skill and grace of the Eskimo jumpers. The jumpers literally looked like they were beginning to fly as they rose in the air in their colorful fur-lined gingham parkas. The highest jumpers were usually women. No one ever gave Jason or me an answer for that. The competition to be the highest jumper was keen, though, and everyone had his or her favorite jumper.

The Winter Carnival was a good place for the Eskimos and Indians to demonstrate some of their traditional native customs for us *Chichacas*. Jason and I watched Eskimo women sit cross-legged on sealskins on the frozen river and chew seal skins to make mukluks, their traditional native boots. These mukluks were made of fur and were worn knee high. The tops of the mukluks were decorated with beaded handcraft, but the sole of the boot was made of durable, long lasting seal skin.

In order to be able to sew the fur and the seal skin together, the seal skin had to be tenderized, and the Eskimos did it with their teeth. The Eskimo women literally chewed the edges of the skin until it was tenderized. Once the edges of the seal skin were tenderized enough to get a needle through, then the two pieces of fur and skin were sewn together with a bone needle made from walrus bone. Jason and I were fascinated by the sight of Eskimo women whose front teeth were nearly worn away to their gums from years and years of chewing this tough animal skin.

At the Winter Carnival, the natives also displayed an assortment of their traditional native arts and crafts. We saw scrimshaw, the delicate hand etched ivory carved from walrus tusks or bone. During the years we lived in Alaska, Daddy and Mama were given several priceless pieces of this unique native art. The scrimshaw from the 40s and 50s is now considered a treasure because much of that scrimshaw was crafted from prehistoric fossils dug up in the construction of local buildings. Today it is illegal to use the prehistoric fossils. Most of today's scrimshaw is made with machines, but in the 40s, scrimshaw was all tediously hand etched by Eskimos during long winter nights in their villages.

It was also at the Winter Carnival that we saw our first displays of Eskimo and Indian beadwork on their mukluks and belts. This work, too, was handcrafted. The Eskimos prepared handcrafted parkas for sale at the Carnival, but these parkas weren't the gingham variety, and they weren't cheap. The Eskimos and Indians knew what the tourists wanted, and they knew that tourists would pay dearly for these coveted souvenirs of the far north. These parkas that the Eskimos sold were made the way we saw them in the books—with the fur on the *outside*.

After our first winter in Alaska, the Winter Carnival became an event that we anticipated as much as kids in the lower forty-eight anticipate the County Fair. Not even the great Texas State Fair in Dallas could compare to the Winter Carnival in Fairbanks!

Chapter 6
The Land of the Midnight Sun

In late April or early May of 1948, amazing changes began to take place in Alaska. Just as the Alaskan winter was harsh and severe, the spring eventually arrived, and how welcome it was—especially after our first winter. We had lived in South Texas all our lives, had played outdoors every single day, and had never worn any outer clothing—not even a sweater. The changes we adjusted to that first winter were countless.

During all our winters in Fairbanks, there was a minimum of three feet of snow on the ground continually from October to April. In the spring of 1948, Jason and I were anxious to get outdoors again and run and play. Finally, after winter sputtered one last time with an April snow, the snow and ice began to melt. From the day when we arrived in Fairbanks in October there had been snow on the ground. Jason and I hadn't even seen our new yard yet; actually, we hadn't seen *any* ground.

Because there is so much snow during the winter in Alaska, it takes many days for it all to melt—even after the weather warms up to 60 degrees or more in the spring. One spring our school had a circus, and I was the "tight rope walker." Mama made me a little costume and umbrella out of pink crepe paper. I was so proud of that costume that I wanted a picture so Mama took me outside, and I posed for the picture against the backdrop of a snow bank. Gramma was really unhappy with Mama for making me stand outside in the cold for a picture. It wasn't cold outside, though; the snow just hadn't all melted yet.

After our first winter, our family had survived nearly six months of snow—snow everywhere, and it took a long time for it to all melt away. All of this snow plus the snow in the mountainous regions, and the frozen rivers, lakes, and creeks eventually began to thaw. The early pioneers had established what we learned was the Breakup Lottery. Toward the end of the long, dark winter a tripod with a clock that registered the day, hour, minute, and second was erected on the Chena River. People from as far away as New York City and beyond placed bets guessing when the tripod would trip.

The clock on the tripod stopped at the precise day, hour, minute, and second that its lever tripped. This was an indication that the river ice had broken and water was breaking through the top of the ice. Spring officially arrived in Fairbanks when the tripod on the river fell, and once again the river began to flow. As spring neared, lottery frenzy grew more intense with each passing day. The person who successfully guessed the day, hour, minute, and second of the breakup won the lottery. As long ago as 1948, this lottery had a jackpot in the thousands of dollars and was one of the biggest lotteries in the world at that time.

The breakup brought an abundance of other changes along with it. In 1948 most of the streets and roads in Alaska were unpaved dirt or gravel. These roads were passable as long as the ground remained frozen; in fact, the roads were easier to drive on in the winter than in the spring and summer. The spring thaws transformed the streets of Fairbanks into muddy floes. Spring floods were common, and it was an everyday occurrence to see a driver standing by the road holding a long stick. We soon learned that this was just another driver who was sounding the depth of the water in the road to see if it was passable.

In Fairbanks—even in the summer—the soil only thaws a few inches. Beneath about twelve to fifteen inches of the Alaskan topsoil, there is always permanently frozen soil called permafrost. Since the soil doesn't thaw consistently, often some pockets of soil thaw deeper than others. This causes the roads—especially roads in the 40s and 50s—to have huge potholes. It wasn't unusual for Daddy to get stuck or to see someone else stuck in the massive amounts of mud and the huge potholes that plagued the Alaska roads in summers and springs.

Getting stuck was a major dilemma. Sometimes it took several people hours and the assistance of additional vehicles to get a car or truck unstuck from axle-deep mud. Once when Daddy got stuck in the Hudson, a truck and then a wrecker also got stuck trying to pull him out of the mud. It was just an ordinary everyday event to get stuck. If Daddy wasn't stuck at least once a day, he was helping someone who was.

Despite the major mud problem, we loved the Alaskan springs. It was fun to see what had been tossed or buried in the snow during the winter. People found all sorts of missing or surprising items right in their own front yards. But what we enjoyed the most were the flowers, the birds, and the beautiful fresh spring air. Spring is wonderful anywhere, but when it has been over six months since

you have been outdoors without wearing layers and layers of clothing, and when you have gone months with only three or four hours of
light in a day, spring is *wonderful.* As the end of May approached,
Jason's school was dismissed for the summer, and we began our first
Alaskan summer adventure.

Fairbanks is within two hundred miles of the Arctic Circle. Just
like the winter days are long and dark, the summer days grow increasingly long and light. By June 21 (the summer solstice) the sun was
shining twenty-four hours a day—a phenomenon called the Midnight
Sun. Because of the earth's tilt, all the Arctic regions of the world have
twenty-four hour days of sun during the summer solstice.

During that first long winter of 1947 and 48, none of us could
fathom seeing sun for twenty-four hours. We were just thankful for
the two or three hours of semi-light that we had during the middle of
the day. The sourdoughs just had to be wrong on this one. But they
weren't! Mama had to hang black pull down window shades in all
the windows of our little house so that we could sleep at night. Jason
and I loved these summer nights with the nonstop sun. We played
and played and played. We were soaking up a supply of sunlight for
the next long winter.

Another extraordinary Alaskan spectacle is the occasional night-
time display called the Aurora Borealis—the Northern Lights
(Appendix No. 2, p. 218). Just like families today visit Disneyland
and view nightly fireworks and sound exhibitions, Mother Nature
sporadically puts on her own sound and light show in the Arctic sky.

When the Northern Lights would surprise us, Daddy and Mama
would summon us kids outdoors, and together we watched an amazing spectacular display—no charge and no tickets. Once you have

seen the Northern Lights, you never forget them. Mama and Daddy were captivated by the Aurora Borealis, and many times during the winters and sometimes even in the summer, we witnessed the Northern Lights.

One unique feature of Alaskan summers always intrigued visiting friends. Since the soil remains frozen solid nearly eight months of the year, it is impossible to dig in the winter. All anticipated digging had to be done during the short summer months when the soil was semi-thawed. Because of these conditions, it was common to see a lot of digging during the summer.

People dug a basement or set a foundation during the summer even if they weren't fully prepared to build the superstructure. The summer digging also included making appropriate plans for winter deaths. That meant that winter graves must be dug in the summer. Going to the cemetery in the summer was really entertaining. Each summer the city estimated how many graves they might need for the next winter, and then (hopefully) they dug enough graves.

Daddy had a standing joke he played on our guests. He would stand down in one of the graves, and tell his visiting friend to take a message back home for him. "Tell them," Daddy would say, "that I've got one foot in the grave in Alaska." One summer Mama took a picture of Daddy and us kids standing in a grave and sent it home to her family. Gramma didn't think that picture was funny either.

Mama and Daddy didn't have much money, but that never stopped us from having wonderful times in the Alaska summers. Picnicking by the rivers with friends was a favorite pastime. Mama would pack a lunch, and the five of us would pile into the Hudson and head to the edge of town to eat along side an icy-cold Arctic river or stream. One of the most spectacular joys of an Alaskan summer is the gorgeous wildflowers. Everywhere the earth is blossoming with wild irises, wild roses, forget-me-nots (the Alaskan state flower) and assorted varieties from the lupine family.

One of these lupine varieties is what the Alaskans call fireweed. Fireweed seems to thrive in the Arctic regions of the world, especially in Alaska. It grows on a stalk two to three feet high, and it has red-toned blossoms that cover the top several inches of the stem. These hearty flowers often blanket entire hills or valleys, and from a distance it really looks like the mountainside or valley is on fire.

Sometimes our summer excursions took us to Livengood or Circle City where we tromped through these historic gold rush ghost towns. We kids tried to imagine what life had been like just a few years earlier when these were thriving cities full of miners, prospectors, dance hall girls, saloons, and assay offices. How different these towns were in the 1940s than they had been just thirty years earlier. When we visited them, they were nearly empty ghost towns with deep-hidden memories of lost dreams and found fortunes.

There was an occasional sourdough that refused to leave, but some of these ghost towns had no inhabitants at all. Often, we joined with friends and their children for one of these summer excursions into Alaska's past. In the evening, we would build a big fire, someone would boil coffee for the grown-ups, and we would finish our picnic or excursion with campfire songs and roasted marshmallows. What a contrast these Alaskan summers were compared to the bleak winters.

Another of our favorite summer activities was berry picking— all types of berries: raspberries, high bush and low bush cranberries, wild strawberries, and everyone's favorite—blueberries. Alaskan blueberries are the best, biggest, and juiciest on the entire continent. Daddy would drive the Hudson to the edge of town and park near a wooded area. Mama gave each of us a berry bucket to carry into the brush, and within minutes we were back at the Hudson with our buckets overflowing with berries—many of them as large as marbles.

Mama collected berries in a larger pail that she kept in the trunk. Within just a short time, we could collect several gallons of blueberries. That first summer in Alaska Mama learned a zillion ways to prepare and cook blueberries. We ate them fresh with cream or ice cream. Mama baked fresh blueberries in cobblers and pies. She froze whole blueberries for the winter. But what she did most with blueberries was to make jam, jelly, and syrup for the next long winter. We soon all agreed that nothing is better than Alaskan berries—fresh, frozen, or in jam.

In Texas Mama hadn't made much jelly or jam, but in the 1940s in Alaska, everyone made jelly for the next winter. Mama quickly educated Jason and me in the process of sterilizing jars, cooking the berries, straining out the pulp for jelly, adding sugar and finally pectin to allow the mixture to gel. I thought that melting the wax to seal pints of jelly, jam, and even syrup was the most fun of all.

Following the summer of 1948, Jason and I shared our basement world with shelves of blueberry, raspberry, and cranberry jams, jellies, and syrups. During the next winter, I cherished my summer memories of berry picking as I gazed at all these colorful jars and glasses that lined the shelves near my basement bed. These blue, red, and pink jars brought memories of the warm days of berry picking during the cold, colorless winters.

There were other wild things that we learned to eat in Alaska. The most unique forest product Mama learned to cook was rose hips.

She learned that beneath the petals of wild roses were rose hips, and these are also good for making jelly. Jason and I picked dozens and dozens of wild roses. Then Mama followed a friend's recipe for rose hip jelly. She boiled the rose hips, strained the pulp from them, added sugar and a slight drop of red food coloring, and finally the pectin.

Dozens of rose hips usually produced only one or two pints of rose hip jelly. This lovely, clear, light pink jelly was a special treat that we all loved. It was an Alaskan delicacy. We didn't know that rose hips were one of nature's best sources of Vitamin C. In 1948 rose hip jelly was just a special treat that we saved for special occasions and important guests.

Mama was from Oklahoma where they liked greens, so she learned to boil and cook dandelion greens. If she did them just right, they were great. But it she didn't, they had a bitter, tough taste. Wild rhubarb grows all over Alaska, and Jason and I would grab a stalk and eat it while we played. Uncooked rhubarb has an extremely sour taste, but we acquired a love for this unusual snack. What we preferred more, though, was the fresh rhubarb pies that Mama made in the summer. Eating "off the land" was new to us, and Jason and I thought it was an absolute amazing adventure.

If we were lucky in our berry picking, we might catch sight of a cache, a unique structure found only in the far north. A cache is a small log cabin set on 12 to 20 foot high log poles in order to keep the cache and its contents out of reach of bears and other wildlife. Since caches were created for the bush and wilderness areas, it was rare to see a cache near civilization. Trappers, Eskimos, Indians, and bushmen built these caches and stocked them with food and provisions, warm blankets, and even matches.

According to the unwritten rules of the wilderness, a cache was never locked. Generally, there was a ladder lying on the ground nearby, but it was never to be left leaning against the cache. It is easy to get stranded, snowbound, or lost in the Alaskan wilderness, and a cache has saved the lives of many hunters, trappers, or hikers who became lost or disoriented in Alaska's wilderness regions.

Alaskan summers (as our family quickly learned that first summer in 1948) had one specific annoyance that no one could avoid. Mosquitoes! They were everywhere, and they were monstrous and huge. No one could get away from them; they bit, and they bit hard. We never left home on any of our excursions without bottles of mosquito repellent. Mama spread the repellent on any exposed body part to try to keep the pesky mosquitoes away. I guess it must have helped some. Jason and I quickly learned that mosquito bites, infections, itching and scratching were just a trade off for the chance to be outdoors in the twenty-four hour sunshine.

In the roaring rivers of Alaska, we were introduced to another Native American cultural device—the fish wheel. The fish wheel—now a federally protected Native Alaskan Indian fishing right—is found only in Alaska. No one (then or now) except native Alaskan Indians was allowed to use the fish wheel. Over centuries the Indians learned that the salmon could provide them with an excellent source of nutrition both during the wonderful Alaskan summers, but more especially during the long, cold winter.

Ultimately, the native Alaskans invented and eventually perfected, the fish wheel. The fish wheel works rather simply, but it is a profound invention. A large paddle wheel similar to those on Mississippi river boats is situated in the current of a swiftly flowing river. As the paddle turns with the moving river, two huge arms scoop salmon from the river. These arms catch the salmon, and as they come out of the water, the fish are thrown into a large basket behind the paddle wheel. A wooden walkway is built from the riverbank across the roaring waters and out to the wheel and the basket. All the Indians need to do is to walk out to the basket and collect the fish. In this fashion, hundreds of pounds of salmon are retrieved from the Arctic rivers.

The Indians' custom was to dry the fish which kept them edible for months and provided a winter food supply both for themselves and their dogs. More salmon was preserved for their dogs than for the Eskimos and Indians themselves. The Indians built birch sapling tripods and set birch pole extensions between the tripods. In this fashion, they dried tons of salmon.

The fish wheels and accompanying drying racks were another crowd stopper with visiting guests. Sometimes Mama or Daddy let Jason and me walk out on the wooden ramp into the river and watch the hundreds of salmon still flopping in the fish wheel basket. I remember gingerly walking across a roaring river on a little wooden walkway to see this basket of fish. What a sight! There must have been several hundred huge salmon in that one basket.

Hunting and fishing have always been a major part of the Alaskan life-style. Daddy wasn't a sportsman, but he liked to cook. Occasionally, he was invited to accompany groups of hunters as they hunted moose, deer, bear, pheasant, or ptarmigan. He became their resident hunting trip cook. Daddy never shot an animal of any kind, and I think he caught a fish only once while experimenting with ice fishing on the Bering Sea near Nome. I don't think Daddy ever really enjoyed the hunting and outdoor "roughing-it" part of these trips, but he did enjoy being with his friends.

Mama was the one who gave our family a great hunting experience. In the summer of 1948, Mama organized a group of teenagers from the church and took them about 100 miles from Fairbanks on a three-day camping trip. No one had ever done anything like this with these teenagers; Mama was young herself, and these kids loved her. Everyone was excited about the trip, and plans were arranged for weeks for this wilderness adventure. They camped beside a river north of Fairbanks and north of the old gold mining town of Livengood. Livengood had a few inhabitants, and the majority of that once thriving village was now a collection of abandoned run-down buildings. The teenagers took all their own tents, sleeping bags, food and necessary cooking supplies with them.

Mama made many plans for the kids on the trip, but she told them strictly: "no guns!" They could fish if they wanted, but being totally unfamiliar with firearms, Mama was not about to be responsible for teenagers with guns. But, teenagers are teenagers whether it's 1948 or 2001. It was always difficult for anyone to get one over on Mama, but one teenage boy snuck a gun along on the trip.

The first night Mama's teenagers camped near a road crew that was repairing some of the many potholes caused by the spring thaw. The road crew told the gun-carrying teenager that a rogue bear was raiding their food supplies and trash. It had been continually harassing them. That's all the encouragement the young man needed. He didn't know Mama very well, though. Without Mama's knowledge, this teenager agreed to shoot the bear for the road crew. Early the next morning while Mama and most of the teenagers were still sleeping, he shot and killed the bear.

He intended to leave the dead bear lying by the side of the road. But, Mama was not happy! And, in her typical style, she was not willing to ignore the teenager's disobedience. Mama was smart, though, and knew that she couldn't afford to have all these teenagers mad at her. When she learned about the dead bear, Mama made the shooter skin and clean it. Then, she let the teenagers roast the hind-quarter. Together at midnight, Mama and the teenagers sat around the campfire and ate roasted bear. For years after that, people were still talking about Mama and the bear.

Our first winter and summer in Alaska was an important mile-stone for all of us. As a little girl I remember a lot of talk about becoming a sourdough. This seemed to be an extremely important right of passage that we absolutely must pass. After our first Alaskan winter and summer, our family were all considered sourdoughs—even baby Sammy.

After one full winter and summer, we were veteran Alaskans, fully ready and prepared for another cold winter. At least that's what we all thought. The winter of 1948-49, however, would challenge our family with events of enormous magnitude. Our first winter in Alaska had been exciting as we adjusted to a whole new world, and our first summer in Alaska had been magical. None of us could imag-ine what lay ahead during the long winter months of 1948 and 1949.

Chapter 7
An Unforgettable Winter

Before we knew it, our first magical Alaskan summer was past, and once again another demanding Arctic winter was looming ahead of us. The fall of 1948 was really an exciting time for me. As long as I could remember, I had anticipated going to school with Jason. Daddy had always read to us, and after we moved to Alaska, there was even more time during the long winter evenings for our reading sessions.

There was no television and little radio in the late 1940s. Therefore, our family spent a lot of time together reading and playing games and telling stories. Daddy read to us often—such books as *Heidi, Bob, Son of Battle, the Five Little Peppers, A Christmas Carol, or Aesop's Fables.* These exciting stories only heightened my enthusiasm for school and all the wonderful doors that would open for me when I learned to read for myself.

When Jason returned to school in the fall of 1948, at last I was old enough to accompany him. Going to school meant that I needed a whole supply of new clothes. The summer of 1948 Mama placed her first biannual order to Sears and Roebucks. When the order arrived, I was in seventh heaven. I had new dresses, skirts and blouses, snow clothes, thermal underwear, and sweaters. I was most proud, though, of my new red boots—perhaps because they came from the Northern Commercial Company downtown and not from a catalogue.

Kindergarten was in the basement of our three-story school, and I was so proud that first day of school as I marched into the school with Jason. I was growing up, and although Jason remained the brightest in our family, school was always easy for me, too. I took to school like a duck takes to water. School was where I belonged. I loved my teacher and thought the new world of cloakrooms and special girls' bathrooms and desks and artwork and music and all that goes with school was absolutely thrilling.

Walking back and forth to school with Jason and the other kids was a brand new experience. We only lived two blocks from the school, but walking with the other kids and my brother was totally different than walking to the post office with Mama or driving to town with Daddy.

About a block from our house was an old sourdough's log cabin. This cabin had only one room with one small window on each side of the cabin. In the middle of the cabin was an old potbellied stove that was probably hauled up the rivers and over the Chilkoot Pass. The roof was made of sod, and additional sod had been stuffed into the chinks between the logs to keep the cabin warm. The cabin was simple, but we kids thought it was awesome. The old prospector had snowshoes, animal traps, gold pans, picks, and shovels lying around everywhere. Most of all, he told amazing stories about the gold rush.

Once in a while, the old prospector invited us into his cabin and told us exciting stories of the gold rush and early pioneer days. Going inside this cabin was unquestionably against all the rules.

Jason and I made certain that Mama never knew about our stops at the cabin. If she had known, it wouldn't have been pretty. We had definitely been taught not to go into the homes of strangers, but we did it anyway because no one knew, and the old sourdough's stories were just too captivating to miss. We thrilled to the almost unbelievable stories the old man told us. He painted word pictures of the gold rush and Alaskan winters before there were towns or buildings that made an indelible impression on my mind.

Even though going to school was exciting, the winter of 1948 held some difficult and sad days for our family. When Mama was expecting the baby in 1947, she and Daddy were so excited about it that they had made the big announcement to Jason and me the day Mama bought the three new dresses. In the winter of 1948, Mama was pregnant again, and I didn't know it. I expect Jason and I were going to be told soon, but things happened before they could tell us. I was home from kindergarten for the afternoon, Jason was still at school, and Sammy was napping. Mama was sitting in our tiny living room in one of the chairs with the drop down wooden arms. I was kneeling beside the chair while she brushed my hair. Suddenly, she pushed me aside and ran as fast as she could to the bathroom.

I knew something was wrong, but I certainly did not know what it was. I was so confused, and I didn't know what to do. Somehow, Mama reached Daddy on the phone, and he came running across the yard from the church next door to the little parsonage. Before that day was over, Mama was in the Catholic hospital, and all three of us were split up and sent to different houses to stay. Things had happened fast, and I was scared.

Mama was really sick and spent five weeks in the hospital. I stayed with some people on the base who had a little boy my age, and although we had fun playing together, I missed Mama, my family, and our little house. After a week, Daddy brought Jason and me back home to be with him, but Mama stayed on the hospital. She came home for a few days and then was readmitted for another week. Mama lost her baby during that second visit, and that's the way Jason and I found out she was pregnant.

After Daddy brought me back home from our friends' house at the base was when my accident happened. One night I woke up myself and everyone else in the little house screaming like crazy. I was six then, and I didn't know what had happened, but I did know that my ear hurt so badly that I could hardly stand the pain. Daddy quickly ran down the stairs to our basement room to see what was wrong. I pointed to my ear and told him how much it hurt.

Daddy couldn't find anything wrong with my ear and thought that I was having a bad dream because I missed Mama. On second glance, Daddy saw something buried deep within my ear canal. Carefully, he reached inside and discovered a bobby pin. The bobby pin had been in my hair when I went to bed, but Daddy didn't know that he should take it out before I went to sleep. I had turned over in my sleep in such a way that the bobby pin was driven all the way through my eardrum.

When Daddy extracted the bobby pin from my ear canal, it relieved the built-up pressure. I felt better at once, stopped crying, and eventually went back to sleep. Daddy went back to bed, and I guess because Mama was so sick, forgot all about that nighttime incident and never took me to the doctor.

Daddy was permitted to take Jason and me to visit Mama only once during her six-week hospital stay. Sammy wasn't allowed at all. Because of this rule, it was at least a week after my accident before Mama saw me. She asked Daddy why I was so quiet and why I had little blisters behind my ear. It was then that Daddy remembered my accident during the night a week earlier. Mama insisted that Daddy take me to the doctor the next day, but by then it was too late. The doctor gave me a penicillin shot which temporarily made me feel better, and Daddy thought it was all over. I had been seriously injured, though, and it would be a long time before my ordeal was over.

Little by little, Mama got better, and at last her long hospital stay was over. We were so happy to have her back home, but we were sad when Daddy and Mama told us there would never be another baby. Mama's strength began to return, but she had one lasting result of that long hospital stay that remained for the rest of her life. During her six weeks in the hospital, there was nothing for Mama to do but read. And so, she read. Her body was just too weak, and all her reading in this weakened condition eventually affected her eyesight. By the next year, Mama was required to wear glasses all the time.

Friends of Daddy and Mama at the church thought it would be good for them to have a little vacation after Mama's ordeal with the baby. They gave Daddy some money and insisted that they go away for a while. After we were farmed out again, Daddy and Mama left on the Alaska Railroad for a week's rest at the lodge at Mt. McKinley National Park.

During World War II the entire Alaskan Railroad system was upgraded, and finally luxurious passenger cars were added. The Alaska Railroad was one of the most modern conveniences in Alaska, and the entire territory was extremely proud of its dependability and modern passenger cars. It was the connecting link for many little villages between Anchorage and Fairbanks, as well as a cargo route for all kinds of supplies.

Then (and now) the train went through Denali—the Eskimos word for the "great one." But in 1948 everyone called Denali Mt. McKinley. Denali is the highest mountain on the North American continent, and on a clear day it is absolutely breathtaking. It always reminded me of a giant meringue pie protruding from the landscape into the atmosphere. At the base of the mountain is Horseshoe Lake, which perfectly reflects the mountain.

Mt. McKinley was part of the U. S. National Park System, and it was proud of its top quality hotel. By today's standards, the Mt. McKinley Hotel wouldn't be top quality, but in 1949, it was the most modern hotel Alaska had to offer. This was Alaska's Five Star Hotel, and the entire territory was proud of it.

Daddy and Mama took their vacation in Mt. McKinley National Park during the coldest part of winter 1949. The park hotel was open for guests, but there were few of them. Daddy and Mama were pampered and treated like royalty since the hotel had a full staff and few guests. After a week at Mt. McKinley, Mama and Daddy felt rested and ready to return to Fairbanks. They were anxious to return home to the three of us and resume normal family life. After Mama's long hospital stay, and our family's forced separation, we all felt like we deserved to settle down to normal.

Mama and Daddy's vacation was extended because of an unusual accident that could happen only in Alaska. The train from Anchorage never arrived at the park to take them back to Fairbanks. That winter had been so cold and there had been so much snow, that wildlife had begun using the plowed train tracks for paths rather than cut their own paths across the landscape. As the train was traveling north from Anchorage towards the park, a moose decided that the train tracks were his own private territory. The moose didn't like it at all when the train appeared on his territory, and so he did what only a wild moose would do. He charged the train and broke its snowplow.

The train was forced to stop until a new snowplow was brought from Anchorage. While the train waited for the new snowplow to arrive, a snow slide completely covered the engine and buried three men inside. The engineer, brakeman, and fireman had to be dug out of the buried engine before the train could continue towards Mt. McKinley. Meanwhile, Daddy and Mama stayed at the hotel two additional days—courtesy of the Territory of Alaska and the National Park System. Finally, the train reached the park with its new snowplow, and Daddy and Mama were able to return home at last. Mama was well, but my ordeal had just begun, and none of us knew how serious my ear problem really was.

While Daddy and Mama were deciding what to do about my ear, we were faced with yet another dilemma. Deep in the winter of 1949 when the temperature was at its very lowest, the main electric transformer for the city of Fairbanks blew out. This caused the entire city to be without electricity, and it created an emergency of catastrophic proportions.

Something had to be done immediately or the entire town would be lost. This was serious. The Federal Exploration Co. had its own transformer, which they offered to Fairbanks as a back up system until the city's transformer was repaired. There wasn't enough power in the FEC transformer, though, to operate the entire city at once. For three weeks Fairbanks was kept alive by an ingenious alternative power scheme.

Fairbanks was divided into quadrants each of which received electric power only two hours at a time. This meant that each quadrant received electricity four times a day for two hours on a rotation system. The times were announced on the radio and listed in the newspaper when each specific area of town would receive electricity. During our two hours periods of electricity, we were specifically instructed to get our homes as warm as possible.

Even though we had hot water radiator heat, our furnace was run by electricity. The furnace in the basement of the church heated the church, our little house, the rent house with the well, and the log cabin. It was imperative that Mama and Daddy keep the house and church warm. Mama bought canned heat called *Sterno*, and whatever she needed to cook was cooked over these cans. Most of our meals during the week's disaster consisted of sandwiches and cold foods. It was romantic and exciting to eat night after night by candlelight, but this was a serious problem. The pioneer spirit of the Alaskan people prevailed, and miraculously Fairbanks weathered the electricity crisis.

Finally, the electricity crisis was history, and we were back to normal. At least everyone was but me. After her long sickness and hospital stay and the relaxing vacation, Mama was back to her normal self, but I wasn't. Each afternoon I ran a low a fever. Mama sent me to kindergarten each morning as usual, but by the time the morning was over, by mid-afternoon everyday I would have a low fever again. The fever was never alarmingly high, but Mama began to really worry about me.

And so, we returned to the doctor. When the doctor examined my ear, he was shocked. It had been at least two months since the night I injured my ear in my sleep. The doctor couldn't believe what he saw. He told Daddy and Mama that my eardrum was completely destroyed, and that it was so infected that nothing could be done about it until the infection was gone.

Doctors today have dozens of different miracle drugs, but in the late 1940s, the only miracle drug the doctors knew to use was penicillin. Even though Alaska was removed geographically from the rest of the United States, medical care was very current and up-to-date because the influence of the military during World War II had made its mark on medical care in Alaska.

The doctor prescribed penicillin for me all right, but not in pill form. For six long weeks Mama or Daddy took me to the doctor five days a week for a shot. The six weeks after that, we went to the doctor three times a week, and then finally we went once a week. After over four months of this, I was pretty shot up. At last the infection was finally gone from my body. Now the doctor could concentrate on some method to repair my destroyed eardrum.

If my eardrum couldn't be repaired either through drug therapy or surgery, he told Daddy and Mama that I would be deaf in my left ear for the remainder of my life. I felt fine after the long ordeal of incessant doctor's visits. Spring had arrived, and all I wanted to do was go outside and play. Mama and Daddy knew, though, that my ear condition was serious and must be treated soon.

The doctor gave Daddy and Mama two options, neither of which he was sure would work. A doctor in Seattle had a brand new experimental surgery in which a new eardrum could literally be transplanted into the ear. This surgery ultimately became perfected, and many years later as an adult, I eventually had that very operation. But in 1948, this surgery was experimental. In addition to that, either Daddy or Mama would have to fly with me to Seattle for the operation.

In 1948, health care was pretty much a thing of the future—there wasn't much health insurance for most families, and Daddy sure didn't have any. The mission board and Daddy's congregation had been assisting Daddy and Mama with some of their medical bills, but they couldn't afford a trip to Seattle in addition to all the hospital bills. Not only did I now have hundreds of dollars of medical bills, but Mama and Daddy still owed for Mama's long hospital stay.

Daddy and Mama opted for the doctor's second choice. He suggested that they take me to Anchorage for a week's stay in the hospital there. The hospital in Anchorage was more modern than the hospital in Fairbanks, and the doctor thought that perhaps they could heal the eardrum with some brand new experimental miracle drugs. He said I would be hospitalized for a week so that I could be monitored. The drugs that I ultimately received in the hospital are common today, and no doctor today would even think about hospitalizing a patient for them. In 1948, doctors just weren't sure of the side affects of these drugs so the hospital was where I was headed.

Jason, Sammy, Mama, and I set off for Anchorage by train. Mama and Daddy had told us about their trip to Mt. McKinley, but now we traveled past Mt. McKinley and on to Anchorage. I thought that trip was the most fun I had ever had. We ate in the dining car, saw the beautiful mountains, lakes and streams. For the first time ever, I saw some of the traditional native villages.

We took the train beyond Mt. McKinley, through the Talkeetna Mountains, over Hurricane Gulch, and across the Susitna River. Tourists now flock to see these sights, but this was just a trip to the doctor for me. We continued south toward the Matanuska Valley—an area of Southern Alaska that grows the most gorgeous vegetables imaginable—and finally into Anchorage.

The trip on the Alaska Railroad covered 356 miles and took us one long, adventurous day. There was one significant missing piece to this trip though. Mama and Daddy hadn't told me why we were going to Anchorage. They must have thought that after all my doctors' visits it would be best to tell me about the hospital at the last minute. I thought we were going to stay with friends in Anchorage who had a little girl my age. In my imagination, this was going to be a fun vacation. She and I would run and play and enjoy the warm climate of Anchorage.

Boy, was I surprised! Mama realized at the last minute that I should have been told about the hospital, but by then it was just too late. I pitched a fit. I hated that hospital; they made me sleep in a crib. It was humiliating. I was six years old, and besides that, I wasn't sick!

In addition to all the other disappointments, the hospital had the crazy idea that kids should only have visitors one time during the week. Mama felt badly about all this and bought me all sorts of coloring books, paper dolls, puzzles, and books. She bought me my first real bathrobe and fancy slippers with fringes made of feathers. None of that made much difference to me. That was the longest, most miserable week of my life.

The doctors weren't sure if this drug therapy could heal my injured eardrum, but Mama and Daddy were certainly willing to give anything a try. Daddy and Mama both believed in prayer, so they and their friends all prayed that God could work through the medicine and restore my hearing. And so I spent one long, lonely week in the Anchorage hospital right in the middle of my second Alaskan summer. Summer weather was so precious to us after the long, cold winter that this only made my stay seem more confining and unfair.

There was little television anywhere in 1949 and none in Alaska. The other kids in the ward and I devised our own diversions to keep ourselves amused. We were never at a loss for entertainment. I quickly discovered that I wasn't the only one who couldn't have visitors. None of the children could. That didn't make any sense to me then, and it doesn't make sense today, but in 1949 the hospital thought this was a good medical practice.

This week in the hospital did, however, teach me some valuable life lessons. One boy in the hospital made quite an impression on me. He was so much fun, but even though I was only six years old and "sick" myself, he made me aware how fortunate and blessed I was. Robert was about nine years old, and during the winter he had been accidentally shot on a hunting trip by his own father. The shot had destroyed his leg, and he was now an amputee. He was the first child my age that I had ever met who was confined to a wheel chair. Robert was familiar with the children's ward because he had been there several weeks already.

Robert was the kid who showed me around and told me which nurses were nice and which ones didn't like kids. Several hours each day he was gone from the ward. Eventually, I learned that he was in therapy being taught to walk with crutches. For a week, the boy in the wheel chair was my best friend—my only friend. Although I never saw Robert again, he taught me that it never helps to feel sorry for yourself, and that there is always someone else who has a more difficult situation than you do. That was an important life lesson for a six-year-old.

When that miserable week was over, Mama checked me out of the hospital. I was so happy to be going home, but we had one last visit to the doctor to endure. At this final examination, the doctor poked his special lighted instrument deep inside my head through my ear canal one more time. My ear hadn't hurt at all since the penicillin treatment earlier that year, but I had to continue to endure these visits and the probing that the doctors and nurses always did to my ear.

The doctor looked into my head, and it seemed to me that he looked forever. At last, he extracted his light from my ear, looked at Mama, and shook his head. "If I hadn't seen this eardrum a week ago, I would never know it was the same ear," he said to Mama. He took a small hot needle and cauterized the ragged edges of the damaged eardrum to rid it of unnecessary scar tissue.

That was it! My ear was healed. Mama was crying when we left the doctor's office. She and Daddy and their friends were sure that their prayers along with the experimental drug therapy had totally restored my hearing and healed my ear. Not once as I grew up did I have an earache, and I never had any hearing loss. My dilemma was solved, and Mama and Daddy thanked God for my healing.

Daddy drove the Hudson to Anchorage to pick us up, and on the way back to Fairbanks, we camped. Our family wasn't big campers, but this return trip to Fairbanks was so much fun after the week in the hospital. Jason, Sammy, and I slept in a bed Mama made in the back seat of the Hudson, and Daddy and Mama slept on the ground in sleeping bags.

Daddy camped by icy, mountain rivers, and we cooked and washed dishes in cold mountain streams. As we drove through the Matanuska Valley and saw the amazing fields of vegetables, it was hard for me to imagine that all this beautiful food could really grow in Alaska. Every mile of the highway from Anchorage to Fairbanks was gravel and driving was slow, but I didn't care. Returning to

Fairbanks that summer and enjoying the beautiful outdoors, I nearly forgot my ordeal in the Anchorage hospital. But not quite!

By the time my hospital ordeal was finally over, it was time to start the first grade. My second summer in Alaska was over. Mama was in good health once again after her winter ordeal with the baby, and my hospital experience was behind me as well. Our whole family had survived a difficult winter and summer. The winter of 1950 was ahead. Little did we know that it, too, would be a "dilly."

Chapter 8
World Events Touch Our Lives...

Even after the end of World War II, there continued to be serious world events in the late 1940s. These events made the whole world nervous. Jason and I didn't fully understand these world events, but ultimately they would directly impact our family immensely. The areas of world unrest that affected our family most were events in the Far East. Alaska is as far west and north in North America that you can travel, but when you travel as far West as you can travel, "West" becomes "East."

For months the world had been listening to rumblings of a brewing crisis in Korea. Communist forces soon took control of China, Chiang Kai-Shek (the Chinese president) fled from China, and the United States stood once again on the brink of a global war (See Appendix No. 3, p. 219). In June 1950 Mao Se Tung led the North Koreans across the 38th parallel and invaded South Korea, capturing the capital, Seoul. President Truman immediately ordered United States ground troops shipped to Korea.

With that decision, the United States was once again involved in a major world conflict. The United Nations called our presence in

Korea a police action, but those of us who lived in Alaska in 1950 called it the Korean War. It seemed strange to me as a small girl that one part of a country would invade another part of the same country. A country is a country, or that's what I thought. What I didn't understand much about was communism. Soon the word *communism* was a concern to everyone in Alaska.

Basically, the way communism was explained to me was that in a democracy the people are given the freedom to speak what they think, own their own land, make their own choices, etc. But with communism, the government owns everything, your children can be taken from you, your work is predominantly for the state, and people are killed or exiled just for disagreeing with the leaders. That is a pretty simple explanation, but I understood it, and it struck terror to my young heart.

Alaska is the closest American soil to Korea, and so we were put on alert. This alert meant many different things. For one thing, military presence in Alaska was everywhere. On Memorial Day and the Fourth of July, the Air Force and the Army came to town in force. There was always a huge parade. Jason and I would stand on the side of the street and watch while hundreds of ground troops and paratroopers in their full battle uniforms marched in perfect precision through town.

These troops were led by a military band and followed by dozens of tanks, military trucks, jeeps, and large mounted guns. Battalion flags, squadron flags, the Alaskan flag, and the forty-eight star American flag would all be waving. It was pretty impressive, and for years I thought that every city in America had the same degree of military presence.

One military exhibition was especially impressive. We were told that Alaska must be prepared for a strike. I learned that a strike was when the enemy—the communists—would attack us. To practice for this possible strike, the Army and Air Force decided to transport an entire unit of the 182nd airborne paratroopers and all their battle supplies from Ft. Bragg, North Carolina to Fairbanks.

They weren't just going to fly to Fairbanks; they were going to land there. And they weren't going to land at the airport in a Pan American passenger plane like we did in 1947. The paratroopers and all their equipment were going to jump from the sky. All of Fairbanks was excited about the big jump day; this was to be a really big deal. Daddy and Mama took the three of us to the jump site to watch this historical event—once in a lifetime, actually. What a day that was!

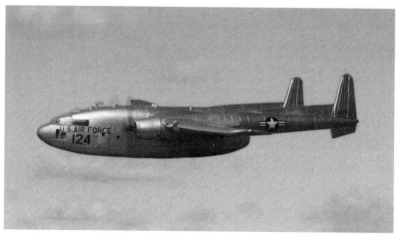

Air Force C-119 - "The Flyer Boxcar"

None of us really knew what to expect, but eventually gigantic Air Force C-119s began to roar from a distance, and then we began to see small dots on the horizon, and finally many huge airplanes were overhead. These planes were unique; they had propeller engines and two tails connected by a cross bar. The whole back end of the plane could open for a drop. The G.I.s nicknamed the C-119s flying boxcars, and that's exactly what they looked like.

Just seeing the planes was exciting, but that initial excitement was only the beginning of a show that no one who was there that day will ever forget. As dozens of these flying boxcars soared overhead, they began to open their giant payload bins, and out of these bins tumbled hundreds and hundreds of paratroopers. Following the men came tanks and jeeps and trucks and supplies of all kinds. Everything and every man had a parachute.

The sky was one giant collage of gorgeous colored nylon chutes as this entire battalion floated to the ground below. Mama took dozens of pictures. What a thrill that day was. As soon as the Army and Air Force were satisfied that this jump could be accomplished, they packed up everything they had dropped and every man who had jumped and returned them to North Carolina. This was one massive drill, and as a little girl it made me feel safe from the dreaded communists.

There was another communist threat, though, that made me feel fear. The communist threat in Alaska during the Korean War came more from Russia than Korea. Russia was an ally of North Korea, and we were perilously close to Russian soil. In fact, Big Diomede Island (Russian soil) and Little Diomede Island (U.S. soil) in the Bering Sea are only twenty miles apart. The Russians had a large military base on Big Diomede Island. It was militarily vital that Fairbanks have the capability to become invisible in case of a night-time raid. To combat the possibility of a Russian air strike, the military ordered that the entire town of Fairbanks conduct regular air raid blackout drills as a precaution against a Russian attack.

Instructions for these drills were given to the entire population, and we were expected to comply. The first signal of an air raid drill was a long, sad, siren wailing and blowing in the night. This was a dismal, foreboding sound, and it was our clue for action. At the sound of the siren, we were to immediately make our houses invisible during the entire time of the air raid drill. If even the slightest light was showing through a window or door, someone was sent to the house where the people were warned to keep their houses dark. When the drill was over, a different sounding siren signaled "all clear."

Fortunately, every home in Fairbanks had black window blinds that were used during the summer nights of the midnight sun. When we heard the air raid siren, Mama and Daddy made certain that all our blinds were pulled to keep the light inside. Then, to be sure we were invisible, they turned off the lights and lit candles. When the "all clear" siren blew, it was then safe to turn our lights back on and raise the shades. Jason and Sammy and I thought these black outs drills were all such fun. Actually, they were tremendously serious, because we never really knew whether the planes roaring overhead were Russian or American. Between 1948 and 1950, those of us who lived in the Arctic regions of Alaska were always in harm's way. In truth, the Russians could have struck us any day.

Surprisingly, the world event that impacted our family the most occurred in China. As soon as we arrived in Alaska in 1947, people in Daddy's congregation began to tell us about two remarkable people and their three daughters and son. They weren't in Fairbanks in 1947 when we arrived; they were in China. They still played a significant role in our lives, however.

In 1936 when it was time for a missionary doctor from Northern China to take his furlough and return to America for a year, he made different plans. In those days, missionaries generally stayed overseas in a foreign country for a minimum of five or six years. After this period of time, the early missionaries returned to the states for a year of recuperation and fund-raising.

When it was time for his furlough in 1936, Dr. Fitz decided not to take a traditional furlough and then return to China as he had done previously. In fact, he wasn't sure if he would ever return to China because of the extremely tense political situation there. Dr. Fitz and his wife set out for Alaska to take advantage of the Homestead Act. He would put down roots on a homestead and wait and see what happened in China.

Dr. Fitz's intention was to be a missionary in Alaska and homestead there for a few years while the political unrest settled down in Northern China. In this way he could provide his family with a future. In 1936, then, Dr. Fitz moved his family to Alaska from Northern China. When I thought about the Fitzs' colossal move from continent to continent, our move from San Antonio to Fairbanks didn't seem so phenomenal.

Dr. Fitz moved his wife and three daughters and young son to the Fairbanks area and spent one unbelievable year digging out an existence on the homestead he claimed just outside of town. The stories people told us about the Fitzs were amazing. In the beginning they lived in tents on their new land, and then they built a small log cabin. Dr. Fitz's first attempt at building a log cabin failed when the cabin literally fell in on itself overnight.

There was a lot to learn in order to survive in this primitive, unforgiving environment. The Fitzs cut down trees and manually drug logs through the brush to clear a road up the hill to their land.

After their first log cabin failure, they learned how to chink the logs properly and built a log house on their land with logs made from their own trees. They planted their first crop of potatoes and vegetables in 1936 and dug a root cellar. As the years passed, the root cellar and the house both expanded until they were spacious and comfortable.

Not only did Dr. Fitz homestead a place for his family, but he also purchased the property in Fairbanks where Daddy's church was standing when we arrived in Alaska in 1947. When he located some available property in Fairbanks, Dr. Fitz contacted the Kansas City mission board and convinced them to purchase the property and start a mission. The only building on the property when Dr. Fitz purchased it was the little log cabin that became the home of the first pastor.

As soon as the land was purchased, Dr. Fitz and some of the church people embarked on the task of constructing a little chapel for their church. A few years before we arrived, the "real" church was erected on the corner of 10th and Noble, and the first little chapel was converted into the parsonage. This little chapel-turned-parsonage was our home for five years.

Because of the war and the political unrest in Northern China, Dr. and Mrs. Fitz's initial stay in Alaska was much more prolonged than they ever anticipated. Throughout the 1940s, marauding hordes from Mongolia continued to advance into Central China from the North, and more and more Chinese fled to the southern area of the country. Once again, communism was raising its ugly head.

Dr. Fitz finally despaired of ever returning to Northern China, but in 1947, a few months before we arrived in Fairbanks, Dr. and Mrs. Fitz returned to Southern China to organize a new mission there.

Their brief stay in Alaska had lasted eleven years, and during those years, they had become local legends. The people in Daddy's little congregation talked about Dr. and Mrs. Fitz with much love, respect, and admiration. They were local heroes.

The Fitzs had just barely begun their missionary work in Southern China when world events forced them to leave China once again. Their return stay to China lasted only one year. When Mao Se Tung forced Chiang Kai-Shek to leave China, all Americans living in China at the time were advised to leave immediately. In 1949, Dr. and Mrs. Fitz were some of the Americans living in China who were warned by the U.S. State Department to leave immediately. They weren't even given time to pack their belongings to take home. The Fitzs were told that they would probably never have an opportunity to return to China. They barely had enough time to get out of China with their lives.

Dr. and Mrs. Fitz grabbed their family picture albums, the few personal belongings they could carry, took a long, dusty train trip across China, and made a quick retreat before China was officially closed to the Western World. Dr. Fitz was an extremely humble man, and he waited in China as long as he possibly could to try to make certain that his Chinese friends were as safe as possible. He and Mrs. Fitz were on the last ferry carrying foreigners that left the mainland of China. From there, they went directly to Hong Kong and caught the first plane to Alaska.

Our dear friends, the Fitzs, were some of the lucky Americans in China. Many American missionaries and civilian workers in China in 1949 were captured by the communists and incarcerated in prison camps for years. In these camps, the Americans (both men and women) were treated inhumanely. Dr. and Mrs. Fitz were grateful that they had escaped and that they had their Alaskan homestead to return to.

The world was really shaky in 1949, and many thought we were on the brink of World War III. In many ways the late 40s and early 50s were a frightening time to be alive, and Alaska was a frightening place to live during this period if you let your mind dwell on the events in the Far East. Knowing Dr. and Mrs. Fitz made world events seem extremely real to Jason and me as we grew up in Alaska during the Korean War.

No one in our family had ever met the Fitzs, but we had certainly heard a lot about them. One day in 1949 Jason and I were sitting on the blue trunk in Mama and Daddy's bedroom reading. Mama was busy with laundry in the basement when the doorbell rang. I was the first one to run to the door, and there they stood. Dr. and Mrs. Fitz were both small people, but they seemed bigger than life to me that day as they stood together in our doorway, both of them wearing long gray overcoats, and looking extremely tired. Instantly, I recognized them. My mouth just dropped as I stared. I had never seen the Fitzs and neither had Mama, but I literally abandoned them standing in the door-way, and ran to Mama. "Mama," I shouted, "Dr. and Mrs. Fitz are here!" That must have seemed a funny welcome for these dear people.

Mama emerged from the basement laundry room and invited the Fitzs inside our little house—the house they knew well since they had built it. Dr. and Mrs. Fitz carried only two suitcases with them—all that they were able to gather in the few hours time they had before they left China. They had come by taxi from the airport to our little house on Noble Street to ask Daddy to give them a ride to their homestead outside of town.

What a trip they must have had from China to Alaska. I was fascinated when Dr. Fitz explained to us that because of the International Dateline, they actually arrived in Fairbanks *before* they left Hong Kong. How grateful we were to have the Fitzs safe in Fairbanks and not in a communist prison camp in China. Daddy drove them to their homestead, and the Fitzs began to rebuild their lives.

The Fitzs' concerns about the political situation in China were real, because when the Fitzs left China in 1949, they never returned. World events had short-circuited their dream, but their lives continued to have a major impact on the world and our young lives.

That day began my love affair with the Fitzs. They became my Alaskan grandparents. Grandparents were one of the few things I missed in Alaska. Gramma was in Oregon, and Daddy's father was in Oklahoma. We only saw them one time in five years. After we became acquainted with the Fitzs, Jason and I spent many wonderful days at their homestead, both playing and learning.

Their house was a log house but much bigger than the little log cabin behind the church and bigger than our little house. It had a large kitchen, a comfortable living room, a bedroom for the Fitzs, and loft bedrooms for their children. Some of the logs had been chinked and plastered on the inside, and Mrs. Fitz had even wallpapered over the plaster. The wallpaper was cracked and yellow, and it had an unforgettable musty smell from being closed up during the year the Fitzs were in China.

Over the years they lived on the homestead, Dr. Fitz had built additional rooms extending from the original log house, and these were covered on the outside with black tar paper. I'm sure he had plans to one day finish his house, but that was the custom in Alaska.

It was not unusual to see finished basements covered with tar paper with an entrance protruding from the flat surface of the future house. Many people lived years in a finished basement before the house above was built. So, Dr. Fitz' tar paper exterior blended with the pioneer décor of early Alaska.

Dr. Fitz loved to farm. He planted acres and acres of potatoes, carrots, and other root vegetables such as rutabagas and turnips on the land that he and his family had cleared many years before. Because Alaska summer days are blessed with the midnight sun, some of the largest vegetables in the world grow there. I remember seeing a cabbage that was three feet in diameter. Dr. Fitz occasionally grew a carrot or turnip that was large enough to win a blue ribbon at the Tanana Valley Fair.

His root cellar was fascinating to Jason and me. A root cellar is a large barn-type structure dug partially underground to keep produce and supplies cool and fresh. Dr. Fitz's root cellar was one of the biggest I ever saw. He could even drive his tractor inside. His root cellar had a large, curved sod roof with grass and flowers growing on it, making it look like a colossal Oklahoma dugout.

Jason and I thought this root cellar was the grandest place in the world to play. Their old homestead was full of Chinese treasures that they brought to Alaska in 1936. There were Oriental vases, wall hangings, and beautiful China dishes. Wow! When we walked through the door of the Fitzs' log house, we were literally in another world.

Mrs. Fitz also was a baker. After Mama lost the baby, she never baked as much as she did at first. But Mrs. Fitz did. While we were outside running and playing over the hillsides of the homestead, Mrs. Fitz was making fresh bread in her big kitchen in her old iron oven.

When we came back inside the log house, the smell of that bread permeated the air. Mrs. Fitz would take her big knife, cut us each a huge slab of bread, and then Jason and I would spread butter and some kind of homemade Alaskan berry jam or jelly on it. Mrs. Fitz's bread was the very best I ever ate.

Dr. Fitz had an assortment of old vehicles and machinery scattered around his homestead. Jason and I loved to play on all the old rusty tractors, pickup trucks, plows, tillers, and nameless other farm machinery. We climbed in the cabs of these vehicles and pretended to be all sorts of people performing all sorts of daring adventures.

The Fitzs' homestead was a kid's paradise, and Dr. Fitz was like most grandfathers. He indulged us and let us play in areas that would have frightened Mrs. Fitz and our parents if they had known. When the days grew long, Dr. Fitz took out his Chinese picture albums and escorted us on a journey far away. These thick albums were overflowing with snap shots of a distance land and culture—each secured in the four corners with little black triangles. They would take us through the albums page by page explaining all the curious sights.

What an education this was. We saw pictures of people in quilted pajama-type clothing and pictures of buildings with odd-shaped curved roofs. We learned from the Fitzs that there are thousands of people in the world who live completely different lives from ours. They taught us how the Chinese people bound the feet of baby girls so that they would remain small—an ancient Chinese sign of femininity. That was the custom that both fascinated and revolted me at the same time.

Dr. Fitz taught us about the Chinese economy as well. He explained to Jason and me that before they evacuated China, the money was worth so little that an entire wheelbarrow full of Chinese paper money wouldn't buy a loaf of bread. The Fitzs loved China and missed it immensely, so these picture sessions were probably as dear to them as they were stimulating and educational to us.

The one thing about China that Dr. Fitz seem to miss the most was *Chinese*. He loved Chinese and had a library of Chinese and English books that he read regularly. Jason and I were enthralled by the funny little Chinese characters that represented words. Dr. Fitz, like Daddy, liked to read aloud to us.

We never understood why the Chinese books started at the back of the book and read from bottom to top. It just didn't make sense. Reading, like nearly everything else at the homestead, became a cultural experience when Dr. Fitz taught us that the English language wasn't the only language in the world.

When Dr. Fitz read aloud, he read in Chinese. Neither Jason nor I could understand a word he was saying, but it was captivating to sit beside him as he held a big Chinese Bible or book and read aloud to us. No one was ever more inspiring than Dr. Fitz when he read from the Chinese Bible. He would open the big book on his lap, locate a section he wanted to read, and then begin to read aloud in his Chinese nasal tones while he followed the strange little characters with his index finger.

We didn't understand Chinese, but somehow, we did understand. To Dr. Fitz, his old Bible represented all he and Mrs. Fitz had dedicated their lives to, and what he was forever forced to leave behind because of uncontrollable world events. Jason and Sammy and I never spent much time with our grandparents while we were growing up, but we weren't deprived. Not in the least. Dr. and Mrs. Fitz were our amazing substitute grandparents, and their wonderful homestead was our paradise. The Fitzs loved us and opened a whole new world of thinking and imagination and adventure thousands of miles from our own home and family in the states and thousands of miles from their beloved China.

Chapter 9
Outside for Christmas!

By the fall of 1949 I was ready to begin second grade, the eardrum ordeal was over, and our family was in love with Alaska. Its extreme cold weather, the pioneer spirit of the people, and the ever-present influence of the military—all of these things seem to stimulate Daddy and Mama. They loved Alaska, and we were just kids—Jason, Sammy, and me—so if our parents were happy, we were happy too. Alaska had become our life. One thing was missing, though. Family!

Little Sammy was now past two years old, I was in the second grade, Jason was in the fifth grade, and none of us had seen our grandparents or our extended family for over two years. In fact, Sammy didn't even know who his grandparents were—he wouldn't have recognized them if he saw them. Mama and Daddy, too, felt like they needed to visit their parents and touch bases with brothers, sisters, cousins, and their family and friends in general. It was time to go home.

One huge problem made going home for Christmas nearly impossible. Money! Daddy was only paid $40.00 a week plus the little parsonage for our family to live. After all the medical bills Mama and I had the winter before, there just wasn't any money for such a big trip. The price of flights to the outside was sky-high in the 1940s.

Today, people in Alaska refer to the *lower forty-eight*, but in the 40s sourdoughs and Alaskans of all kinds called anything beyond the boundaries of the Territory of Alaska the *outside*. Over fifty years later it sounds odd to refer to the states as the *outside*, but in 1949 we never gave the term *the outside* a second thought. It was an everyday word in every Alaskan's vocabulary.

Daddy and Mama began to try to devise a plan for our family to go outside for Christmas 1949. The general church held its biannual meeting in Kansas City in January 1950, and Daddy was searching for a way that he and Mama could attend. If we could just get outside to Seattle, we could go to Gramma's in Oregon for Christmas, and then travel on to Oklahoma and Texas. From there, Daddy and Mama could drive to Kansas City. This trip was almost too enormous for Jason and me to even imagine.

The Fairbanks mission was interested in buying a new vehicle for the church's use, but there was no way in 1949 that someone like Daddy could afford to buy a new car in Alaska. The mission board in Kansas City really wanted Daddy to come outside also for their January meeting. Daddy, the mission board, and Daddy's little con-gregation designed an ingenious plan for our family.

The solution was simple: The church would purchase a new car for us to pick up in Seattle. The board wanted Daddy to travel from church to church telling about the mission work and raise money for the mission like he did in 1947. After the board meeting in January, we would drive the new vehicle home. This way, the Fairbanks mission would avoid the unbelievably high shipping charges it cost to get a vehicle into the territory. All of this was a match. Daddy could attend the mission board meeting and pick up the church's new car all at the time.

Daddy began to search for inexpensive plane tickets to Seattle. We were so excited. If Daddy and the church could work all this out, we would really be with Gramma for Christmas. Daddy would hold Alaska services on the way to Kansas City telling people about our Alaskan adventures. He and Mama would leave us in Texas while they attended the January board meeting, and then we would drive the car back to Alaska in February 1950. That was the plan, but none of us knew the adventures that this plan would present to us over the next two and a half months.

The first thing Daddy did was shop for a new car—long distance! He sent for brochures about cars and studied them meticulously until he decided what would be best for us and for the church. Finally, he and Mama settled on a brand new 1950 Ford station wagon. The car was prepaid by Daddy's church, and we were to pick it up when we arrived in Seattle. Once the model, color, etc. of the car was chosen, Daddy shopped some more. This time he was shopping for an inexpensive way for the five of us to fly to Seattle.

In 1947, the general mission board purchased our plane tickets on the finest passenger plane available, but they would not pay for any more flights for at least three more years even though they wanted Daddy at their board meeting. If we went outside, Daddy had to figure out a way to pay for it.

After much search, he found a good flight, but certainly not an ordinary one. In 1949, we flew outside a totally different way than we flew in 1947. Our family hitched a flight outside on a military plane. The price was a mere pittance of what Pan American had cost two years earlier.

This plane was designed for paratroopers and was painted the traditional army camouflage green. Rows of benches for the para-troopers to sit on before they jumped from the plane lined the walls. Down the center of the plane, there was a short row of about a dozen seats. Instead of a passenger door, there was a huge bay from which the paratroopers jumped.

The Army needed this plane in Seattle, and so they were flying it outside empty. Our family sat in the row of seats down the middle of the plane. There were no paratroopers—only our family and a few G.I.s who caught a free flight home for the holidays. There were no flight attendants, there were no reclining seats, there were no fancy little bathrooms, and there was no food.

In 1947 Pan American had served us a tasty lunch on nice little lap trays complete with china and silver. In 1949 Mama packed our lunch. We didn't care, though, because we were going to Gramma's for Christmas. All this flight was to us was an inexpensive lift to Seattle, and Daddy took it. What an incredible trip. Living in Alaska was a continual adventure, but the flight on the paratrooper plane was one of the biggest adventures we had.

When we arrived in Seattle, Daddy's friend met us at the mili-tary airfield. After a night's rest, Daddy set off to take delivery of the new car. As a first grader, I thought that new car was the most gor-geous new car I had ever seen. Our new 1950 Ford station wagon had wooden panels on the side—"woodies," they were called. Our woody had two large doors, and the spare tire was in a special container attached on the back of the station wagon. Having the spare tire on the outside of the car created more room for us inside. The back seat folded down, and there was even a third seat. That station wagon was to become our home and constant companion for the next two months.

I had seen the pictures in the brochures when Daddy was selecting the car, but I never imagined how wonderful this car would be. It seemed so much more modern than the 1946 Hudson. It was sleeker and more air-streamed, and it traveled at speeds over 50 miles an hour. Our family was really getting modern.

1950 Ford "Woody" Station Wagon

By the time Daddy signed all the papers for the new Ford, picked us up, and loaded all our things into the back of the station wagon, it was nearly 5:00 PM. After two years in Alaska, Daddy had adapted to the milder pace and fewer cars on the Alaskan roads than he had been accustomed to in Texas. He was not prepared for what he faced on Highway 99 heading south from Seattle.

We drove away from Seattle right into the middle of Boeing Aircraft rush hour traffic. After frequent delays and countless attempts to maneuver the station wagon into the traffic, Daddy finally got the Ford onto Highway 99. It was extremely difficult for Daddy to adjust to outside traffic, but nevertheless, we finally made our way out of Seattle. Longview, Washington was our first night stop outside.

Mama planned a big surprise for Gramma that Christmas of 1949, and neither Mama nor her sister told Gramma that we were coming. After we spent a night in Longview, and Daddy got rested from the wild Boeing rush hour traffic of the previous day, we continued south toward Medford and our family Christmas celebration and Gramma's big surprise.

We drove 417 miles south on Highway 99 from Longview to Medford, Oregon. Highway 99 was the most modern highway on the West Coast in the 40s and 50s, but it was different than today's Interstate highways. It was modern, but it still bisected every city and town along the way. Our route took us south through Vancouver, Washington, across the Columbia River, and into Portland, Oregon. From Portland we continued through Salem, Eugene, Roseburg, Grants Pass, and a dozen other smaller towns until we reached Medford in Southern Oregon.

That day seemed to drag on and on forever. Logging was one of the main industries in the Northwest during those days. More than once, our new station wagon was stuck behind a logging truck hauling the biggest logs I had ever seen. Some of these logs were so large in diameter that only three or four of them would fit onto one logging truck. It was difficult to pass these trucks on the winding, two-lane roads. This only slowed our progress to Medford and heightened the anticipation of seeing Gramma.

For over two years we hadn't eaten in a restaurant even one time. As we drove south, we stopped by the side of the road and ordered hamburgers, and Daddy even let us splurge and buy milkshakes. This was just too exciting. It was difficult for Jason and me to determine whether we were excited about being outside, the new car, Christmas, eating hamburgers at a roadside restaurant, or seeing Gramma.

At last, we arrived at my aunt's house near dinnertime. Aunt Fran, Uncle Ed, and my cousin Valerie lived in a small two-bedroom house, but it was still bigger than our little house in Alaska. Aunt Fran had dinner ready when we arrived, and in her living room stood the most beautiful Christmas tree I had ever seen. But, Gramma wasn't there.

As soon as we arrived at Aunt Fran's house, she called Gramma and invited her to come over for dinner. Gramma lived near Aunt Fran, but she worked hard all day herself, and Mama's younger brother still lived at home with her. Generally, Gramma didn't go over to my aunt's house until the weekends. Aunt Fran had to do some fast-talking that evening to even get Gramma to agree to come by for a few minutes. Jason and I were getting so excited; we wanted to see Gramma.

Finally, Gramma showed up at Aunt Fran's, grumbling all the way. Then, she saw us. Gramma was absolutely speechless and began to cry. We had definitely surprised her! Suddenly, she wasn't tired at all and stayed at Aunt Fran's for hours. What a wonderful Christmas 1949 was for all of us—especially Gramma.

When Christmas was over, Daddy had established an exhausting travel and speaking schedule for us. He would hold Alaska services as we drove toward Texas and Oklahoma. The purpose of these services was to inform the people back home about his work in Alaska and to raise money for the mission. After we left Medford we traveled south on Highway 99 toward Southern California. Each night Daddy stopped in a different town or city where he had arranged what Jason and I came to call an "Alaska service."

At first, this life style was exciting, but after a few days, it became tedious. We settled into a pattern. Daddy drove most of the day until we arrived at the next town for an Alaska service. At each stop we went to someone's home for a meal, and then all five of us went to church. After the Alaska service, we were sent to someone's home for the night. The next day we began the cycle all over again. Not once did we stay in a motel. That was just too expensive.

Mama had become an excellent photographer during our first two years in Alaska taking dozens of pictures with her new Argus C3 slide camera. For the Alaska services, Mama and Daddy arranged these pictures into sections, and Daddy wrote a dialogue to accompany them. They prepared pictures of scenery, wild life, the dog sled races, Eskimos and Indians, buildings, summer and winter scenes, the church buildings, and our schools.

The final picture each night was a time-released photograph of the midnight sun taken on June 21—the longest day of the year. In Alaska, the sun never sets on June 21; it just dips a tad and then rises again. Daddy's dialogue was always the same as he ended with the statement that "the sun never sets on the work of the church." Daddy had a poetic streak, and he always concluded by telling the crowd that his was the farthest north church of his denomination in the world. It was pretty impressive. At least it was for the first two or three nights.

Jason and I devised many different schemes to keep our selves amused during those long days of travel. There was certainly a lot to see. And a lot that was different than Alaska, but the hours in the car still stretched on day after day. We had almost forgotten about the palm trees in the Rio Grande Valley until we saw palm trees in Southern California. We were astounded when we saw lemons and oranges actually growing on trees. For over two years we had hardly seen an orange, much less eaten one. Now we could pick one from a tree. This seemed impossible and too good to be true. All of us—especially Daddy who did most of the driving—were stunned by the amount of traffic. San Antonio had a lot of traffic, but nothing like the traffic in Southern California. After two years in Alaska, we all felt like the outside was a totally different world. And it was!

Jason and I spent our days in the station wagon playing typical kid car games. We competed to see who could find the most different state car tags. Or we played the game where we looked for a line from a billboard that began with each letter of the alphabet. And we sang. Daddy favored church songs, but Mama taught us wonderful old ballads and folk songs handed down to her from Gramma. Whatever they sang, though, Mama and Daddy's singing seemed to harmonize beautifully with the humming of the tires along the highway. Altogether, this singing created a soothing sound on a weary day.

Once we saw our first Burma Shave ad, we were hooked and began to look for these everyday. They were our favorites. Burma Shave ads consisted of a series of four or five little signs placed beside the road, each of them several hundred feet from the one before. Each sign had only few words of a little jingle printed on it. For example:

(Sign 1) Around the curve
(Sign 2) the car went whizzin',
(Sign 3) The car was hers but,
(Sign 4) the funeral hisin'.

The final sign always said, "Burma Shave." Even Mama and Daddy looked forward to these Burma Shave advertisements. It was a big moment in the station wagon when someone spotted a Burma Shave ad. We all laughed and laughed at these silly little jingles. They weren't very sophisticated, but they broke up the monotony of a long day's drive.

The thing Jason and I liked to do the best, though, was to mimic Daddy's Alaska slide narration. Since each night Daddy presented his slides in a different church, his dialogue was always the same. We got so good at reciting his narrative that we could almost perfectly replicate Daddy's Alaska speech. Jason and I always got real dramatic when we reached the end of his speech and the part about the midnight sun. I think Daddy and Mama enjoyed hearing us mimic them, and they thought we were funny. We just had to have something to do to while away the long, long hours in the station wagon.

In Southern California, Daddy turned the station wagon east through Arizona and New Mexico. Earlier, Daddy had driven us through Yosemite Park in Central California, and now we visited Joshua Tree National Monument and the Mojave Desert. In Arizona, we toured the Painted Desert and even the magnificent Grand Canyon. Each day our rigorous driving schedule continued, because we had to be in a different town and church for another Alaska service. Daddy went out of his way whenever possible, though, so that we could see some of America's natural wonders.

After days of endless driving, and dozens of nights in strangers' homes, we finally arrived in Oklahoma. Since Mama and Daddy were both from Elk City, they had many relatives to visit there. It was good to be able to get out of the car and visit people that we at least vaguely remembered from two years earlier. Little Sammy was a big

U.S. Trip
Christmas 1949

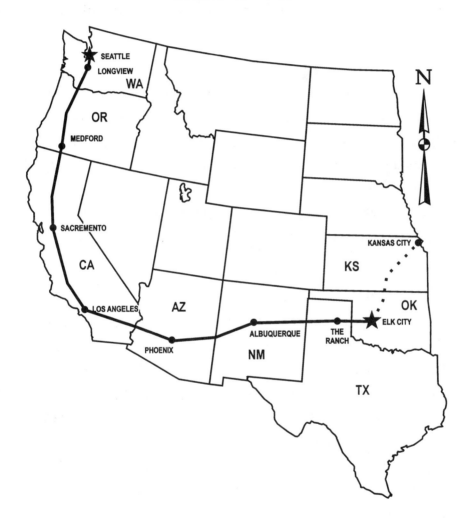

After Christmas of 1949, our family drove down the West Coast and across the Southwest. Each night we stopped in a different town where Daddy conducted one of his "Alaska services." He showed pictures and told about our life in Alaska. After nearly two weeks, we arrived in Oklahoma. Daddy and Mama went on to a convention in Kansas City and left us with Aunt Ruth and Uncle Bob on their West Texas ranch.

hit with the family everywhere we went. He had been so tiny and new when we left for our big Alaskan adventure that many of the family thought Daddy and Mama should wait until he was older. Now, Sammy was a healthy, happy two-year old, and everybody just loved him.

The second week of January 1950, Daddy and Mama drove further east to Kansas City to attend the mission board meeting. This wasn't a meeting for kids so we were left at Daddy's sister's ranch in West Texas. Uncle Bob owned a large ranch in the Texas Panhandle close to Elk City, and that is where we stayed. Alaska and Aunt Ruth's ranch were poles apart. This week with Aunt Ruth and Uncle Bob became another big adventure for the three of us.

Our little house in Alaska seemed like the latest in modern conveniences compared to Aunt Ruth's ranch. The closest town to the ranch was over thirty miles away, and that town only had about 800 people. Once you turned off the state highway, the ranch was several more miles down a dirt road. The ranch stood alone in the country with no neighbors; it was remote. Other than driving into town in Aunt Ruth's pickup truck, the only other connection to civilization was an old crank telephone hanging on the kitchen wall. There was no running water, and Aunt Ruth had electricity at only certain times each day. Near the house was a cellar for protection from a tornado, and near the cellar was the outhouse. There was no bathroom.

In Alaska we never saw farm animals. Now, animals surrounded us all day long. There were chickens and pigs and horses and cows. There were coops for the chickens, pens full of muddy pigs, and a horse trough stood in front of a large barn. The horses particularly frightened me. Uncle Bob's father had been drug to his death by one of their horses the year before, and Aunt Ruth scared me nearly to death with her stories about finding his body out on the plains with one foot still stuck in a stirrup.

Every morning Aunt Ruth got up early and cooked a huge breakfast of eggs, bacon, hot biscuits, fried potatoes, and sliced tomatoes for Uncle Bob and their teenage son. There was a butter churn and a cream separator in the corner—neither one placed there for decoration. Aunt Ruth actually used the separator each morning to separate the cream from the milk.

During our week at the ranch, Jason and I devised a game that we took back to Alaska with us and played again and again. We learned to make our own treasure hunts. This was so much fun. One of us would hide clues around the house and ranch that the other would have to follow until he or she got to the end. At the end we hid some kind of a little surprise. This took up hours and hours of time, and we both loved it and got quite clever with our clues. This world of the ranch was so different from our Arctic world that it was hard for us to compare.

One day on the ranch, I had a big scare that was more frightening than I realized. I was playing outside the front door where Aunt Ruth usually fed the chickens. There were four wooden steps that led down from the door to the dirt yard around the ranch house. Suddenly, I spotted a snake under the steps. Alaska has no snakes at all, and it had been a long time since I had seen a little garter snake in San Antonio. I screamed bloody murder and stood frozen in my tracks.

Aunt Ruth came running from the house. There was a look of terror in her eyes when she saw the snake. She quickly darted to the back door and returned with a hoe. In one swift, experienced movement, she swung the hoe and chopped off the snake's head. It wasn't a harmless garter snake; it was a copperhead! A bite from a copper-head is exceedingly poisonous and can be deadly. Years later, Aunt Ruth told me that the snake spit at her, and his venom made her sick even though he didn't strike. What a week that was!

After a week on the ranch, Daddy and Mama returned from Kansas City to collect us. Just like we had done in 1947, we said our final good byes in Elk City to all our family and commenced our journey north to Alaska. This trip was not going to be like the one we took to Seattle two years earlier.

This time Daddy planned to drive the new station wagon with all five of us all the way home to Fairbanks. None of us had any comprehension of the adventure that lay ahead over the next three weeks or how close to the edge we would come more than once during that time. Our trip north in the station wagon would be a trip to remember forever!

Chapter 10
The Alcan Highway in Winter

Like our 1947 trip from San Antonio, our 1950 return trip to Alaska began in Oklahoma after we said "good-bye" to family. As the days of travel became weeks, our 1950 trip made the 1947 trip pale in significance. We left Elk City, Oklahoma in early February, and Daddy began to wind our way north and west as he conducted Alaska services each night.

By February, Alaska services were routine for Jason and me. Both our 1947 and our 1950 January trips of Alaska services were still recent memories, but these services seemed to be about the only similarity between the two trips. In 1950 we were not headed for Seattle and a comfortable airline flight home via Pan American Airways. Daddy was determined to drive our new station wagon all the way home to Fairbanks, and in the winter—a distance of over 3,000 miles, across wilderness, ice and snow.

Daddy and Mama's family thought this trip was foolhardy, and many of their friends agreed. They said it was unsafe, that the weather was too severe, and they accused Daddy of putting us in harm's way. We would just be too vulnerable to the elements of weather, they said, and everyone agreed that we probably wouldn't make it alive. None of these warnings stopped Daddy or Mama. Jason, Sammy, and I had no idea what all the fuss was about. After our recent trip down the West Coast and the trip to Alaska in 1947, another long trip didn't seem extraordinary. By now, all three of us were veteran travelers.

Southwind
Car Heaters

$29.75

HEAT IN 90 SECONDS!

Just a Few Left

Call Us
At 138

SERVICE ELECTRIC CO.

*Car heaters –
an expensive
necessity in 1947*

Mama and Daddy fully understood the dangers of such a trip and wisely took some valuable precautionary measures. In addition to the factory installed car heater, Daddy had another heater called a *Southwind* heater installed under the dashboard of the Ford. This devise ultimately helped save our lives. We weren't aware of this when we started, though. In addition to winter clothes, Daddy stocked the station wagon with several large heavy quilts, a Coleman stove, additional antifreeze, and an extra ten-gallons of gasoline. As our trip progressed, at least two of these factors worked together to save our lives.

Daddy also purchased a new winter gadget for the windows that was advertised to stop ice from forming inside the car. People today would laugh at his purchase, but in 1950 the defrost system in cars wasn't perfected like it is today. This gadget was an insert of specially treated plastic that Daddy stuck on the inside of the wind-shields. In theory, it was supposed to keep moisture from freezing inside the car. It was advertised to help alleviate visibility problems in case of an ice storm. Later in the trip, this gadget nearly cost all five of us our lives. But, that is later.

Like we had done in 1947, we said our tearful "good- byes" in Elk City and began driving west through Colorado. This time we were not driving to Oregon and Washington. In the winter of 1950, Daddy drove north through Wyoming, Idaho, and Montana. He drove due north from Pocatello and Idaho Falls, through Powell, Wyoming, and Great Falls and Shelby, Montana. Finally, we crossed the international border into Alberta, Canada. This was really desolate country, and it was winter. Many events of that trip are still very clear in my memory, and it's easy to understand why. Our 1950 expedition up the Alcan Highway during the coldest month of the year was unbelievable. Every new day held a new adventure.

Slowly, day after day, Daddy maneuvered the new Ford station wagon north. Each night we stopped in a different town where we stayed with more strangers. And each night Daddy repeated the Alaska slide and lecture routine. When we left Powell, Wyoming, our plans were to drive from Great Falls to Shelby, Montana and then into Canada. The weather dictated our first change of plans that day, and this was an omen of much to come.

A warm *Chinook* wind came up suddenly in the area near Great Falls and melted much of the snow. This sudden change in the weather caused the highway between Great Falls and Shelby to flood. As quickly as the warm wind came, though, the temperature immediately dropped below freezing. This created a highway of ice between the two towns, and the highway was closed. Because of the glare ice on the highway, Daddy was diverted from Great Falls to Cut Bank, Montana. From there we were able to drive on into Shelby.

In February 1950 (after we had been driving in the states for over a week already), just north of Great Falls, Montana, at last we passed through the small town of Shelby—*The Gateway to Alaska*.

On a little state highway that today is Interstate 15, our family crossed the international border in the new station wagon and entered Canada. We revisited Canada many times after that. Except for our Whitehorse fuel stop in 1947, this was the first visit to Canada for all five of us. That was more than fifty years ago, and that first visit to Canada still remains the most memorable and vivid for all five of us.

Our journey through Canada and into Fairbanks would last for twelve more days, but none of us knew it the day we drove through *The Gateway to Alaska* at Shelby. The further north we drove, the more severe the weather became. The temperature dropped from 10 below zero, to twenty below, and then continued to fall.

The mercury on the thermometer never rose above thirty-five degrees below zero anywhere we were for the rest of our trip and the next three months afterwards. Daddy didn't act worried, and Mama was always game for a new adventure, so none of us kids had any fears. We continued our trip north into Alberta, Canada, and Daddy held his last two Alaska services—one service in Calgary and another in Edmonton.

Daddy's service in Calgary was on Wednesday evening. The night before, we stayed in a roadhouse rather than with people from the church. This was a big treat for us kids. After staying in so many strangers' homes, this night in a roadhouse was a blessed change. Although we were unaware of it then, that night in Calgary would be our cleanest and safest and best night's lodging until we reached our little house in Fairbanks eleven days later.

The pastor's wife at the Calgary church was more concerned about our driving to Alaska than anyone we had met so far. Her urgent anxiety about our traveling the highway in winter seemed

U.S. - Alcan Highway
February 1950

Day 1: Elk City - Trinidad
Day 2: Trinidad - Denver
Day 3: Denver - Powell
Day 4: Powell - Shelby
Day 5: Shelby - Calgary
Day 6: Calgary-Edmonton
Day 7: Edmonton-Dawson
   (MP #1 - Alcan beginning)
Day 8: Dawson - Ft. Nelson
   (MP #300)
Day 9: Ft. Nelson - Rancheria
   (MP #635)
Day 10: Rancheria - Whitehorse
Day 11: Whitehorse - Silver
   Creek Lodge (MP #1053)
Day 12: Silver Creek Lodge -
   Burwash Landing (MP #1093)
Day 14: Burwash Landing -
   Tok Junction (MP #1380)
Day 15: Returned to Tok Junction
   after accident
Day 16: Tok Junction - Fairbanks
   (MP #1523 Alcan end)

funny to me. Calgary was freezing, and the thermometer was well below zero. I just didn't understand why our trip up the Alaska Highway was such a big deal for her. She continued in her protest and concern about our safety and finally insisted that Mama take her fur coat. This dear lady would not take "no" for an answer. Consequently, Mama left Calgary with a black fur coat. The coat certainly kept Mama warm, but more importantly, giving it to Mama made our hostess happy.

After we left Calgary and Edmonton there were no more Alaska services. Daddy just aimed our new station wagon north for home and our little house. Hundreds of cold and treacherous miles lay ahead of us. The road itself is legendary. Until World War II there had been no road at all to Alaska. In order to protect the United States from the Japanese, the military was adamant that a ground route to Alaska was as vital to national security as air stations and navy posts. In response to this urgent national need, the 95th Regiment of the U.S. Army Corps of Engineers began building the Alcan Highway—the Alaska Highway—in 1942.

The Alaska Highway was completed in 1943, a record for road construction under any circumstances but phenomenal considering that the road was built in the Arctic. By actual count, 10,607 G.I.s worked 24-hour days in frigid weather—as low as 79 degrees below zero. Even today, the Alcan Highway is considered one of the most spectacular engineering endeavors completed in the Twentieth Century. The "road" (as the workers called it) officially begins in Dawson Creek, British Columbia, and winds a path north through the Yukon Territory and culminates in Fairbanks.

There are over 1,200 miles of Canadian highway from the border to the official beginning of the Alaska Highway at Dawson. From

Dawson, the highway stretches north for an additional 1,523 miles. Our family, then, traveled nearly 2,800 miles of Canadian and Alaskan highways before we ever reached our little house in Fairbanks.

During the construction phase of the highway, there were no places for the road crews to stay. Every single item the G.I.s needed to build the road was transported to each construction site from hundreds of miles away. Life in the road camps was harsh, and the G.I.s barely eked by with the barest provisions. They were forced to sleep in tents in subzero weather and eat battlefront rations. This was a rough, grueling life that made men from boys.

The G.I.s who built the highway had to haul all their equipment north over some of the roughest terrain in the world. This included fording perilous rivers, traversing some of the highest mountains in North America, and negotiating severe mountain grades. It was war, and the U.S. demanded a road link to Alaska; that was all there was to it. There are countless stories and legends of death, frostbite, loneliness, and isolation during the road's construction. No one was ever sure which stories were true and which were just legend developed and nurtured by G.I.s in the road camps. Regardless, a lot of blood, sweat, and sacrifice went into the building of the Alaska Highway.

The entire 1,523 miles of the Alcan Highway is built on permafrost. Permafrost is exactly what it sounds like—permanently frozen earth. In the Arctic, the soil never totally thaws. It remains frozen twelve months a year. In the spring and summer months the earth thaws a few inches or feet in patches beneath the surface. Underneath, however, the earth is always frozen solid.

Even the flat areas of construction were difficult to construct since the frozen soil had to be continually blasted. As the top layers of earth thaw in the spring and summer, the highway becomes more treacherous then than in winter. This thawing creates immense pot-holes—some big enough to destroy a car. The old-timers jokingly called the highway the "Oilcan Highway" because so many cars were damaged driving it—especially in the summer months. In the sum-mer of 1949 one of Daddy's friends drove up the Alcan Highway with his family. His car hit a pothole so large that he broke the axle on his car. Daddy didn't want this to happen to our brand new station wagon. The extreme cold of the winter kept the road frozen, elimi-nating the possibility of potholes.

The fact that the roads were smooth in the winter and easy to drive doesn't mean much now when the majority of the highway is paved, but it was a big deal in 1950. In 1950 the entire highway was gravel or just plain dirt. The Alcan Highway was a very primitive road, and a long and challenging one. Despite the weather, Daddy had chosen the best season of the year to drive it since winter driving guaranteed no potholes. Our trip, though, was not without danger.

Daddy was aware of these difficult traveling conditions when he planned our trip for February rather than during the summer. Until 1948, the highway had been used for military purposes only, and it had been open to civilian traffic just two years when we drove it. This meant, Daddy told us, that our family would be one of the pioneer families to drive the entire highway.

Being a pioneer didn't mean much to Jason and Sammy and me when we commenced the trip. But by the time we completed the journey home to our little house in Fairbanks, we all were well aware that we had really accomplished a significant feat. It was indeed a major undertaking for Daddy and Mama to take our family on such a trip, and they didn't take the responsibility lightly.

The soldiers who built the road had documented for posterity specific events and sites of its construction by placing a milepost at every mile of the highway. Like travelers of the Alaska Highway today, in 1950 we marked the days and events of our trip by these mileposts.

And so it was on a cold, clear day in Dawson Creek, British Columbia, we passed Mile Post Number One at the beginning of an icy, frozen highway. It had been nearly two weeks since we left Oklahoma. At last, with nearly 2,000 miles of driving between Oklahoma and the Canadian border, and another 1,200 miles between the border and Mile Post Number One, we were finally on the Alaska Highway! But we certainly weren't home. After we spent the night in Dawson at Mile Post Number 1, we began our official journey on the Alaska Highway. The Canadian highway authority advised Daddy to put on chains, and he did. About twenty miles past Dawson Creek the chains flew off the station wagon. Daddy took them off, and we never used them again on the entire Alaska Highway.

In 1950 there were few chain hotels and motels even in the lower-forty eight, but there were none on the Alaska Highway. There were no tourist books to research the next cozy little bed and breakfast spot; there were no 800 numbers to call for reservations, and there was no Internet to check availability of housing in the next town. In fact, there seldom was a "next town." This was indeed the frontier.

Travelers on the Alaska Highway were very few, so we were compelled to be totally reliant on fellow travelers and on word of mouth information. To ignore the road gossip could mean certain death. As we progressed north on the highway Daddy listened carefully to news of the road and current weather conditions wherever we stopped. Southbound travelers kept northbound travelers informed of road and weather conditions that lay ahead, and vice versa. We depended on one another!

Decent places to eat or sleep were recommended by total strangers, and their word became gospel. Mama especially kept close track of this information. None of these places was top quality. Not at all! Top quality was out of the question. The questions of the road, rather, were: "Which place is the least offensive place to stop?" Or, "Which place has decent restrooms?" Or, "Where is there at least a passable cook?" And sometimes, Daddy and Mama didn't have a choice about where to stop. It was either stop or die.

It is an intriguing part of Alaska Highway history how places to eat, sleep, and purchase fuel evolved. Even now, the highway winds through a colossal wilderness In 1950, the Alcan Highway was the extreme end of the earth. As the road moved north during its construction , various camps for the road crews were hastily set up along the route. When the highway was completed, it still required a lot of maintenance. Consequently, these camps slowly became small communities. Very small. Sometimes as small as one family. As the road crews built the highway and moved north, occasionally an individual stayed behind to provide provisions, etc. for replacement G.I.s and workers. These houses and camps became known as roadhouses.

Some of these roadhouses developed extremely colorful reputations, with equally colorful operators. You certainly couldn't refer to the roadhouses of the Alcan Highway as *The Nation's Innkeeper*. These rugged individuals had fallen in love with the land, or they felt trapped there—one or the other. As the highway opened and was frequented more often, these lovers of the north simply opened their doors to travelers.

Mama and Daddy were as discrete as possible in keeping Jason, Sammy, and me sheltered from much of the roadhouse clientele. As a rule, the roadhouses had no finesse or cutesy little décor or advertising gimmicks. They provided a warm bed (clean was optional), sometimes a warm meal, a restroom, and that's about all. By noon each day, Mama and Daddy began discussing the current road gossip report about the nearest acceptable place for us to spend the night or eat. This was always a topic of major importance. Some days we were forced to stop driving much earlier than Daddy planned because a particular roadhouse was the best one within a hundred miles. On the other hand, Daddy might be compelled to drive several additional hours before we arrived at the next suitable roadhouse.

Unbelievably, each night Daddy and Mama managed to locate a place for us to sleep. Some nights we all slept in the same room. One night Jason and I slept on the couch in the roadhouse living room, but Daddy always found a spot for us. Our meals were shared at a common table with fellow travelers, G.I.s, road crews, and assorted other forms of humanity. Night after night, we never could predict what kind of a situation we would find ourselves the next day.

Just as the midnight sun shines twenty-four hours during the summer solstice, so the Arctic winter months provide very little sunlight. As a result of this phenomenon of the Arctic, the majority of our 1,523-mile drive north on the Alcan Highway and the 1,200 miles between Shelby and Dawson were driven in semi-darkness.

The further north Daddy drove, the closer we moved toward the North Pole, and as we drew closer to the North Pole, the days grew darker and darker. It was as though we were driving inside a ping-pong ball, and we became as accustomed to this shroud of murky darkness as was humanly possible. There was little traffic on the

Alaska Highway in February 1950, and the horizon remained continually dim and gloomy.

The days grew long, tedious, and monotonous. There were no billboards or Burma Shave ads to keep us amused like there had been two months earlier in California. There were no hamburger stands or restaurants to stop and eat and then play a tune on the jukebox. Most of all, there was little human connection. It was just the five of us slowly inching our way north toward our little house in Fairbanks.

The Little America that appalled us so much in 1947 would have been a welcome vision of delight on the Alaska Highway in 1950. Our family was alone in the station wagon, hour after endless hour. The nights in the various roadhouses provided all of us an opportunity for human companionship from these long dreary days of ceaseless travel. We began to understand how the early pioneers must have felt crossing the vast American prairie one hundred years before. We, too, were pioneers!

One imperative but unwritten rule of the Alaskan Highway in 1950 was simply this: travelers must adhere to the buddy system and always travel with at least one other vehicle—whether you knew the drivers or not. It was just too cold, and there were just too many unknowns to travel alone. At the refueling and lodging sites Daddy always found a vehicle or two to buddy up with. There were no strangers on the highway. By necessity, we became friends.

After we spent the night in Dawson at Mile Post Number 1, we began our official journey on the Alaska Highway. That first day on the highway was eventful. We crossed the Peace River Bridge at Mile Post Number 35. This bridge collapsed in 1957, but in 1950 it was the longest bridge of the entire highway. Jason and I were mesmerized as we peered down at the frozen river hundreds of feet below.

Fort St. John was eight miles further down the highway. In 1950 Fort St. John was a small, rough settlement for highway crews. Daddy didn't stop; he didn't think it was safe. Perhaps, the most memorable site of that first day on the Alaska Highway was Mile Post Number 148—suicide hill. This was the most dangerous hill of the entire highway and more men and animals had lost their lives there than anywhere else on the road. Road crews had put up a sign that read, "Prepare to Meet Thy Maker." I knew what that meant, and I was frightened.

At Mile Post Number 191 we crested the second highest summit of the highway—Trutch Mountain Summit (4,134 feet high). Mile Post Number 300, historic Fort Nelson, was a construction home for 2,000 troops. Less than ten years earlier when the road began, Fort Nelson was the starting point for the road to Whitehorse. Daddy and Mama chose the roadhouse at Fort Nelson for our second night. It was a pretty rough place, and Mama was appalled at how unkempt our room was.

Day Two of the Alaska Highway was more of the same: At Mile Post Number 392 we crossed a 4,250 high summit—just a few feet higher than Trutch Mountain. Beneath this summit was a beautiful frozen lake, which the construction workers had creatively named Summit Lake. Muncho Lake at Mile Post Number 456 was the next major point we passed that day. Since workers were forced to cut their way through the lake's rocky banks and use horse-drawn boats to haul the rock away, it had been one of the most grueling sites for the construction crews. Road gossip reported that Muncho Lake was one of the most reliable refueling stops and checkpoints.

Beneath the frozen Alaskan permafrost there are fabulous natural hot springs. The Army discovered such a spring during the highway's construction and named it Liard Hot Springs—Mile Post Number 496. This was one of the points of interest of Day Two. Regardless of whether the weather is sixty degrees below zero or seventy degrees above zero, the water in these springs is always boiling.

This was just one of the many contrasts of the Yukon and Alaska. Roughly one hundred miles north of Liard Hot Springs we reached Contact Creek at Mile Post Number 588. Finally, at Mile Post Number 627, we crossed the border from British Columbia into the Yukon Territory. Jason and I were both certain that any minute we would catch a glimpse of Sgt. Preston and King.

Beautiful Watson Lake is just across the border in the Yukon Territory at Mile Post Number 635. We drove a few miles past Watson Lake, and at last, Daddy stopped for our third night at Mile Post 710, Rancheria. We had just spent a week on a real ranch in Texas, and this remote spot was nothing like Aunt Ruth's ranch. Nevertheless, Rancheria looked pretty good to us. In 1947 Rancheria opened as one of the first real lodges on the highway, and it was a small improvement from the roadhouses where we had stopped the previous two nights.

On Day Three we pressed on toward Whitehorse—the territorial capital of the Yukon. Road gossip rumored Whitehorse to be a real town, and all five of us were excited to be nearing some semblance of civilization. Daddy promised us that he would rent a room in a hotel in Whitehorse. Our family would stay alone for a change.

Our drive to Whitehorse on Day Three was plagued by a severe ice storm. These storms were one of the many hazards of winter driving. When there is moisture in extremely cold air, the moisture freezes and literally forms ice particles in the air. This is the cause of frost bitten lungs, and that was why Mama always insisted that we wear a wool scarf over our mouth and nose in the winter.

Driving in an ice storm is particularly critical because the little particles of ice seem to just hang in the air making visibility extremely limited. Daddy drove into Whitehorse in an ice storm that made visibility virtually nil, and it was nearly impossible for him to see to drive. I remember watching him lean forward over the steering wheel and get as close to the windshield as he could in order to see the road. (Before the trip was over, I would see Daddy do this again, and that time it would be a matter of life and death!)

For such a small town, Whitehorse had an unbelievable number of road signs. Signs pointed to Upper, Middle, and Lower Whitehorse. Daddy got confused trying to read the highway signs, the city signs, and look for a place to stay all at the same time—all in an ice storm. At last, Mama and Daddy located a little hotel and rented a room.

After the tension of trying to decipher the many road signs while driving in the ice storm was past and we ate some dinner, Mama and Daddy laughed and said the town should be renamed "Whitehorses." We spent our fourth night on the Alcan Highway in a run-down hotel in Whitehorse. The highway had already presented us some amazing experiences, but unbeknown to us, the most critical and challenging adventures lay ahead.

As we drove away from Whitehorse on Day Five, the ice storm was worsening. We all knew that there were no more real towns until we finally reached our little house in Fairbanks. We also knew that there were still hundreds of miles ahead, and the temperature was falling rapidly. It was beginning to snow profusely, and the wind was howling as we drove away from Whitehorse.

At one point during the next four days, the temperature dropped to 75 degrees below zero. The warmest it was for the rest of our Alcan Highway trip was 50 below zero. Most of the time, the temperature hovered at 60 degrees below. It was cold! And the drive was lonely! There were no billboards, and the few road signs that were posted were difficult to read because of the semi-darkness and icy conditions. The next several days of driving in the Arctic would try us all and take our family to the brink of death and back again.

Chapter 11
Snowbound by the Lake

The morning we left Whitehorse it was bitter cold and at least sixty-five degrees below zero. For the first time on our journey, the wind was beginning to blow with a fury we had not seen on this trip. Until that day, even though the weather had been severe, it had been still and dry. We had witnessed some snowfall, but generally the weather had just been bitterly cold. The weather was changing, and we could feel it even inside the station wagon. Daddy and Mama insisted that we wear sweaters and warm clothes even inside the car—just in case!

Our first sign of civilization that day was Haines Junction at Mile Post Number 1016. From Haines Junction there was 160 miles of highway leading southeast toward the coast of Alaska. This highway spur had also been built during the frenzy of the Alcan Construction. It was built as an access road for troops to get to ships off the Southeast Alaskan coast.

Daddy stopped at Haines Junction to refuel, and we went inside a little cafe there for a breather and to get a little lunch. More importantly, though, Daddy wanted to learn about road and weather conditions ahead. It was reported that a blizzard was headed our way, and it was probable that the road ahead might be closed soon.

Regardless of the travel advisory, we drove on toward Mile Post Number 1053—Silver City. The name Silver City was misleading, for all that was there was one good size roadhouse. The roadhouse was beautifully situated on the shores of Lake Kluane, a lake that must be a lovely lake in the summer, but in the winter of 1950, it was foreboding.

Daddy stopped at Silver Creek Lodge on the shores of Lake Kluane for the road condition report. He was told that the severest blizzard of the winter was coming our way, and that the road heading north was open but may soon be closed. Daddy and the two vehicles we were traveling with all decided to risk it and see if we could possibly get ahead of the storm. We didn't go far, though. Just a few miles beyond the lodge, a huge drift divided the highway.

It would have been easy to turn around right then and there and head back for the lodge at Silver Creek, but the code of the north wouldn't allow it. Through the storm and barely visible through the snow drift, we spotted a south bound vehicle on the other side. We were within safety, but they weren't, and we couldn't leave them out there in the elements alone. Mama bundled the three of us up, and we got into the car of two women who were traveling with our caravan. This way we could save the warmth while Daddy and the male driver of the other car with us tried to help.

The driver of the stranded vehicle on the north side of the drift fought his way on foot through the storm to the safety of our little caravan. Just as he was safe and we were ready to turn around and head back to the lodge, another vehicle approached the drift from the north. That driver, also, must be rescued. At last, when Daddy was comfortable with the fact that all the stranded drivers were safe, we turned and headed back toward Silver Creek Lodge.

It had been over two hours since we stopped at the lodge, and now we were back—for the duration. Daddy and Mama bundled us all up to walk from the station wagon to the lodge. It was so cold that we could have suffered frostbite just walking from the car to the roadhouse without all these clothes. It was bitter cold; there was a blinding snow, and a blasting wind was blowing across the frozen lake. Already massive snowdrifts were forming against the side of the roadhouse and anything else that was stationary. These drifts were building to record heights—ten and fifteen feet. At this rate, the road-house would soon be buried in snow. We were in for a siege.

That night there were only the three cars from our little caravan plus the two drivers we had rescued from the highway who stayed at the roadhouse. Mama and I shared a room with the two women who were driving the highway alone, and Daddy, Jason, and Sammy shared another room. That was all the rooms they had. The roadhouse was warm, the room was fairly decent, and we were all thankful to be inside and safe from the elements.

In the morning the storm had only intensified. During the day and with each passing hour, another car or truck dead-ended at the roadhouse. Soon, the roadhouse was bulging with travelers—travelers of all ages, but mostly men. Sammy was definitely the youngest person there, and we were certainly the only children. There was no television or video games—just hours and hours together in a crowded remote roadhouse near the Arctic Circle with more and more strangers arriving hourly. While people kept stacking up in the roadhouse, the snow stacked up outside, and the wind wailed with a fury seldom experienced by man. This was a storm and a half!

Bedtime created unbelievable challenges for the roadhouse operators. In reality, nighttime never arrived because it seemed like night all day because of the dismal weather. There simply was not enough sleeping space for all the weary travelers at Lake Kluane. Most of the travelers carried sleeping bags like Daddy and Mama so all available sleeping bags were brought into the lodge.

People slept on the floor or wherever they could find a spot. Fortunately for us, we had been there the previous night and were able to keep our rooms from the night before. These rooms had no keys, so Daddy and Mama watched us carefully. No one knew anything at all about the other people in the roadhouse. Daddy and Mama just wanted to be careful.

The next day in the roadhouse came and went like the first. More cars and trucks arrived, and with the arrival of each additional vehicle, the food supply dwindled. Generally, people packed food in their cars. All available food was brought into the roadhouse and shared with the other stranded travelers, but there still wasn't enough to go around. There was no way to get supplies into the roadhouse, and there was no way to get out—either north or south! We were stranded and running out of food. Then, the unbelievable occurred.

Several times each day all the stranded drivers at the lodge had been starting their cars and letting them run for a while. This was the way of the north—especially in a blizzard. To let your transportation sit idle meant that it would freeze, and then when the weather did lift, you would still be stranded. Periodically, Daddy and the other drivers bundled up in their winter clothes and braved the storm in order to start their cars. Some of the drivers just took their batteries out of their vehicles and brought them into the roadhouse. Daddy did this often at home in Fairbanks so this seemed common to me.

A big Caterpillar was setting beside the roadhouse when we arrived. The summer road maintenance crew had left this machine at Lake Kluane to be used during the next summer work season. They would return in the spring when the weather and the Caterpillar thawed to use it to grade and repair the road. In the middle of the storm, the Caterpillar seemed dead and worthless.

Toward nightfall of the second day, a bus approached the roadhouse heading north. No one could believe it when we saw it coming. A bus? Where in the world did a bus come from in this isolated place? And what in the world would happen to us now with even more people in the roadhouse? We all knew, though, that this bus load (whoever they were) would be allowed to share the little bit of shelter that Silver Creek Lodge provided. In reality, what we all thought was a strain to the roadhouse, turned out to be our escape route.

This was 1950. The bus carried a unit of Canadian soldiers. Their commander entered the roadhouse and demanded to know about the road conditions of ahead. When he was told that the road was closed, he refused to take "No" for an answer. Instead he said, "Gentlemen, this is war, and the Army must go through!"

His job as commander was to lead this bus load of Canadian troops on Arctic maneuvers. Conditions in Northern Canada are certainly similar to conditions in Korea, and this was an ideal spot to prepare troops for winter warfare. I was just a little girl, but I heard him make his demands; he was emphatic and insistent. It was indeed memorable to hear and see that Canadian army commander demanding that the road ahead be cleared.

By necessity, Alaskans have a spirit of community and a willingness to help one another—stranger or friend. No one knows when he or she might be the next person stranded, so everyone is willing to pitch in and help when there is a need. One man in the roadhouse spoke up and said he knew how to operate a Caterpillar, but no one had the key to the idle machine by the roadhouse.

Key or no key most of the men in the roadhouse agreed that the Caterpillar probably wouldn't start anyway since it was so cold and hadn't been run in months. The Canadian Army commander was insistent that someone at least try. Finally, some adventuresome men attempted to hotwire the Caterpillar in an attempt to get it started. After several coughs and spits in the freezing weather and blasting wind, the Caterpillar sputtered, groaned, and came to life.

The weather was gray and gloomy, both inside and outside the roadhouse. When that Caterpillar came to life, those of us inside the roadhouse were revived as well. The drivers decided that now was the time to make their move. Beyond Lake Kluane the snow and subzero weather continued with Arctic fierceness, but the drifting was not as severe. The wide openness of the frozen lake provided the wind an open pathway to form snowdrifts. There was nothing to stop the drifting—no trees or natural land formations. Most of the drivers determined that if they could just get away from the shores of Lake Kluane, it would be possible to proceed along the highway.

And so, late in the evening of the third full day at Silver Creek Lodge at Mile Post Number 1053, the stranded lodge occupants— including our family—began to come to life again. Starting the station wagon periodically had paid off because when Daddy went outside with the other drivers to start the station wagon, our new Ford turned over on the first try. When the car was warm, Mama bundled up the three of us, and we ran the short distance to the car.

All the vehicles at the lodge formed a caravan behind the Caterpillar. What a parade we made! The Caterpillar was in the lead, plowing a path through the drifts. It plowed just one lane, and the snow piled up ten to twelve feet high on either side of the road as the Caterpillar plowed a virtual tunnel through the snow. We kids thought this was great fun, but Mama and Daddy must have had some fears. "Was this the right thing to do, or should they have stayed at the roadhouse?"

At the head of the parade and immediately behind the Caterpillar was the bus load of soldiers. They really didn't care who was behind them; they just had to get on with the job of practicing war. Each driver must have shared similar concerns and fears that Daddy and Mama had. The continual winter darkness only deepened in this tunnel of snow, but after several hundred yards of the tunnel, we discovered that the weatherman was right. The road was more clear and open as we got away from the lakeshore.

It was approximately 9:30 P.M. when we joined the parade leaving Silver Creek Lodge by Lake Kluane. We had been stranded there over forty-eight hours in a ferocious blizzard. It was a tremendous relief to be on the road again. If Daddy and Mama were worried, they didn't let us know it. After nearly two weeks on the road since we had left Oklahoma, we were all anxious to get home to Fairbanks—regardless of the weather. When we turned away from the lake, the drifts subsided, and soon we were on the open, frozen highway again. We tried to stay together with other travelers because by now the mercury on the thermometer had dropped below seventy degrees. One small mistake or human error and we would all be gone in a matter of minutes.

Eight miles from Lake Kluane, we passed Soldiers' Summit at Mile Post Number 1061 where just five years earlier the highway was officially opened. It was almost impossible to see anything—even the little sign marking the spot of the Highway's opening was obliterated by snow and ice.

By the time we reached Destruction Bay at Milepost Number 1083, the storm had resumed the same fury that we experienced the two days before when we were snowbound at Lake Kluane. When the Alcan Highway opened in 1945, the engineers set up relay stations approximately every 100 miles, and Destruction Bay relay station at Mile Post Number 1083 was the next milepost we passed that night.

At Destruction Bay Daddy acquired the usual road condition report. Ten miles beyond Destruction Bay was Burwash Landing. Burwash Landing had a roadhouse where we could spend the night. Daddy was advised to get us to Burwash Landing as quickly as possible because another storm even fiercer than the one we had been experiencing was rapidly developing.

Around midnight of the third day after we were stranded at Silver Creek Lodge, our Ford station wagon pulled into Burwash Landing at Mile Post Number 1093. Daddy rented the only room available. It was a bad one—one of the worst of the whole trip. It was well after midnight by the time we got settled, and even Mama was actually happy with the poor accommodations. At least we had a place to sleep. In over two days, we had only traveled forty miles, but we were at least moving again, and we were heading north toward home and our little house. All of us were greatly relieved to be out of the crowded lodge. Somehow we thought that surely the worst part of the trip was behind us. But we were sadly mistaken!

Chapter 12
Buried Alive

In the Arctic winter, it's a challenge to keep track of the time of day since there is hardly any sunshine. It could have been early morning or late afternoon when we drove away from Lake Klaune, but it was actually about 9:30 P.M., and it was dark outside. Mama and Daddy had a mixture of emotions when we left the roadhouse at Lake Klaune.

On the one hand, it was wonderful to be traveling again and away from the overcrowded roadhouse. On the other hand, the weather conditions were deadly. It was colder than sixty-five below zero, there were few cars on the highway, and an ominous icy haze hung in the air.

By now, Mama and Daddy and the three of us had all had our fill of the Alaska Highway. We all wanted to get home—the sooner the better. We drove away from Burwash Landing on a cold, dreary Friday morning. The distance between home and us was now narrowed to a margin of possibility. We were on the home stretch. Daddy was determined to make it back to Fairbanks by Saturday so that he could preach on Sunday.

In less than three years, Alaska had indeed become our home, and all of us were homesick for our little house, our friends, and the people of Daddy's congregation. Besides that, everyone back in Fairbanks was anxious to see the station wagon they had purchased. Two good solid days of driving would get us there with time to spare. There were only 425 miles of the highway remaining. Even if we had to slow down for another ice storm, surely we could drive that distance in two days. We would definitely be home by late Saturday evening.

The night we left Lake Kluane was bitter cold, and somewhere after we passed the Donjek River Bridge at Milepost Number 1130, a ferocious wind began to blow. Other than the blizzard at Lake Kluane, we had experienced little wind on our journey, but this wind blew with an unbelievable velocity and occasional deadly gusts.

As we rounded a curve in a mountainous region, the wind howled down through the ravines. Quicker than we would imagine, it caught under the hood of the station wagon. Right before our eyes, the hood doubled back against the windshield. We were shocked. There was no way that Daddy could see. Fortunately, he was driving slowly enough that he could stop without an accident.

We were still traveling in the same small caravan of three vehicles. Immediately, both of the other two vehicles stopped to help us. Together, the three drivers tackled the bent hood. Using all their combined strength, they bent the hood back so Daddy could at least see to drive. They tied it securely in place, and we continued our journey.

Daddy and Mama both were disappointed that after all we had been through that our new car was damaged—and so near to home at that. But a seriously bent hood wasn't going to keep them from finishing the trip. The hood could be repaired in Fairbanks. Our goal now was to get to our little house as soon as we could.

Friday's drive was cold and tedious. Despite the setback of the hood incident, we had a collective song in our heart. We were almost home. Then we were beset by yet another hazard of northern travel. The car began to sputter and gasp and jerk. It acted like it was out of gas, but Daddy knew better than to let that happen. Once again, we were blessed by the company of our companion travelers because the Woody finally just stopped. Daddy and Mama were noticeably concerned, and so were Jason and I. Little Sammy, though, thought it was all a game and kept saying, " Daddy, Do it again."

The Ford had gas, but apparently at the last fueling spot Daddy had gotten some water in the fuel lines. The gas tank was less than half full, and the water in the gas was freezing. We were in serious trouble. Daddy poured our emergency five gallon reserve of gas into the tank along with five gallons from one of our traveling buddies. One of the other drivers had heard of a refueling spot about fifty miles ahead. With much prayer, our little caravan limped into that desolate spot nearly two hours later.

For fifty miles our Ford lurched and stalled and sputtered, but at last we made it to a refueling spot, only to discover that they were completely out of gas. Our dilemma wasn't solved; it was worse. We couldn't go back, so Daddy poured the five gallons of gas from the third vehicle into the Ford, and the three vehicles in our little caravan continued north. We were told that there was another spot just a few miles north that had fuel; with luck, we would make it. We did. Daddy filled the car and the auxiliary gas can, but he didn't call it luck. He knew that his prayers for our safety had been answered.

That night we stayed at a roadhouse in Tok Junction. Our accommodations seemed to be getting worse, and the roadhouse at Tok was the worse yet. We were all certain that the next night—Saturday—we would be in our own little house. We were headed home—bent hood and all. Our little house wasn't much of a house, but it was home, and the anticipation of being back home was growing with each hour on the road.

On Saturday morning somewhere between Tok Junction and Delta Junction, Daddy lost sight of both of our two traveling buddies. We had been together since Silver Creek Lodge, and they had been our source of rescue twice the day before. Apparently, they had turned off the road. One of the unwritten rules of the highway was to never allow this to happen but to always stay within sight of another vehicle.

Daddy wasn't sure how we were separated, but we were so close to home that nothing could possibly happen now. Daddy just kept on driving. If there was another vehicle heading for Fairbanks at Delta Junction, he would buddy up for the last 98 miles home. If not, we would just drive on home alone. We had only a short distance to travel, and Daddy knew we would make it safely.

The weather had remained merciless ever since the blizzard at Lake Kluane. When we left Tok Junction, it was well below sixty-five degrees below zero, and another ice fog had settled around us. The dreary darkness created mental confusion. It was nearly impossible to accurately track time or space. The only time of day that anyone could really tell for certain was the middle of the night when it was pitch black. The rest of the time—anytime of the day—always looked the same. Gray and dismal and cold.

And so we drove—so close to home! But the ice fog was the worst we had experienced on the entire journey. While we crept along at only thirty miles an hour, Daddy was leaning forward with an ice scraper, scraping ice from the inside of the windshield. It was that bad. The little gadgets that Daddy had purchased for the windows to make Arctic visibility possible were worthless.

Since the ground was totally frozen during the winter, road crews simply drove down the highway and plowed the drifting snow away from the road. This created a smooth, drivable roadway. Along each side of the highway at intervals of about fifty feet, they placed tall red poles as shoulder markers to indicate to the drivers where the shoulder of the highway would be if it were visible.

Suddenly it happened! When it was all over, Mama said that she saw what was happening, but she knew she saw it too late to warn Daddy—so she said nothing because she thought she might make our dilemma worse. In his effort to see the road ahead, Daddy lost perspective of the red poles along side the highway, and he began to veer to the right. Before he realized what was happening, we were all goners. Daddy just kept driving between two of the nearly invisible poles, but there was no highway beneath us. He drove the car off the highway, off the shoulder, and into a wide, deep ditch.

The feeling of having no highway beneath a car is one that you never forget. Momentarily, we were suspended in space, and then the station wagon began to settle smoothly into the snow. Time moved so slowly that it nearly came to a halt as we descended together into the eerie, darkness of the snow.

The station wagon sank until the entire car with the five of us inside was buried under the snow. Even though Jason, Sammy, and I were just kids, there was a quiet awareness among us that this was serious. Time was of the ultimate essence. Daddy knew instinctively that he must act immediately or we would soon all be frozen beneath the snow.

The first thing Daddy did was say a brief prayer and ask God to give him wisdom that somehow we would be delivered from almost certain death. Then, Daddy went to work doing what he could do. He found the flashlight and lit the Coleman camp stove to give us some warmth. Daddy knew not to let the flame burn very strong because too much flame would quickly dwindle the amount of oxygen in the station wagon. As a result, the stove didn't emit much warmth.

We already had on coats and sweaters, but quickly Mama helped us find our hats and mittens. Jason and I wrapped up in the sleeping bags Daddy had brought along for emergencies, and Mama wrapped little Sammy in a quilt and held him closely in her lap. After Daddy was certain that we were as warm as possible, he set out to get help.

Very cautiously, Daddy began to roll down the driver's window. This was a difficult task because the pressure of the snow from the outside and the freezing conditions of the road before we went off the highway made it next to impossible to budge the frozen window. Daddy wasn't sure how far we had descended in the snow, but he and Mama both agreed that we were probably not very deep. When Daddy began to try to roll down the window, the extreme cold actually worked in our favor. It was so cold outside, and the snow was frozen so solidly, that it stayed in place like a wall and did not fall inside the car.

Daddy was keenly aware that the only chance for our rescue was for him to get back onto the highway and just hope and pray that a vehicle would drive by soon enough to see him and help him rescue the family. Because of the ice storm, we hadn't seen a sign of another vehicle of any kind for over an hour. We were literally all alone under the snow in unforgiving weather, and yet we were within driving distance of our little house.

How ironic these last days of our long journey had become. The whole episode was uncanny. For nearly two months all we had done was travel. Daddy had driven the new station wagon thousands of miles over all kinds of roads and in all conditions. Despite everything that had happened, we had remained safe. Now, with home nearly in sight, we were in serious, life-threatening danger. Something had to happen soon or it would just be too late. Chances were strong that if we were not rescued within the first hour, we probably wouldn't be discovered until spring.

When Daddy began to pull himself out of the station wagon, none of us knew what to expect or if we would ever see him again. We were at the mercy of fate, and even as a little girl, I was conscious of this fact. We were helpless and alone. Fully bundled in all his own winter wear, Daddy began to laboriously pull himself up and out of the window of the station wagon. When he did, Daddy soon realized that he and Mama had been right. The roof of the car was parallel with the road. That is what saved us. The snow was just too frozen and too heavy for Daddy to tunnel through much of it so the fact that we weren't very deep in the snow was indeed a blessing.

Daddy must have been quite a sight as he hauled himself through the window of the station wagon. He was covered with snow and ice as he climbed over the shoulder of the highway. Just as Daddy climbed onto the highway, a large truck loomed on the horizon. Through the haze of the ice storm, the truck driver saw the dim form of a man climbing onto the highway from the ditch. That was Daddy! The truck driver was witnessing Daddy's emergence from our family's frozen tomb. At first, he must have thought that the vast whiteness of the north was playing tricks on his eyes, for it is not uncommon to become disoriented when everything is the same color—white. This is called snow blindness and it's real.

Of course the truck driver stopped. That was the rule of the road—you always stopped to help someone in distress. Buried in the station wagon beneath the snow, Mama and the three of us couldn't believe our ears when we began to hear muffled sounds above us. Now, we thought that our senses were playing tricks on us. It was the miracle that Daddy had prayed for.

The truck driver and Daddy dug through the snow until they reached the rear bumper of the car, and together, they attached a heavy chain to it. And just like that—with Mama and my brothers and me still inside the station wagon—we slowly began to feel ourselves being drawn upward from our icy tomb. Within less than thirty minutes of Daddy's prayer for our safety, we were being rescued.

But now, our situation was precarious. As the truck pulled, the station wagon slowly began to grind its way backward through the snow bank and up onto the highway. The four of us had been buried in the car for over a half an hour when at last all four tires were firmly on the frozen highway. It was urgent that we get to some warmth—and immediately! The station wagon doors were frozen solid, but the truck driver and Daddy worked with all their joint strength until they pried them open.

As quickly as the station wagon doors were open, the truck driver and Daddy rushed Mama, my brothers, and me to the warm truck cab. How great that dirty old truck cab felt. We were safe; we were warm; and we were together. What a blessing! The station wagon, though, needed attention. It was just a big white, icy frozen form of a vehicle—certainly not operable.

There was no way we were going anyplace in that frozen car, and so our plans of proceeding home that night were dashed. The only option for us was to load into the cab of the truck, tow the station wagon, and return to Tok Junction. Tok had a small garage, and the station wagon could be worked on there. And so, after two days of being snowbound in a blizzard by the frozen lake and then being rescued by the Canadian Army, and after having home in sight, we were headed in the opposite direction from Fairbanks.

To our surprise, there was nothing mechanically wrong with the station wagon. Because the snow bank had softened our descent, there was no damage to the body of the vehicle either. The engine, however, was frozen solid, and it took one entire day to get the car thawed out and running again. Our trip north on the Alcan Highway was becoming a never-ending marathon.

A day after we left Tok Junction the first time, we again set out for Fairbanks. It was Sunday morning when we left Tok; we were definitely not going to make it home in time for church. Daddy's little church always had services on Sunday night as well as Sunday morning. Maybe, just maybe, we would be back in time for the Sunday night service.

Daddy was even more determined now to get back by Sunday than he had been two days earlier. We were all tired, the weather was brutal, and we were claustrophobic from being in the station wagon so many days. We were sick of the rugged housing arrangements we had been forced to endure and tired of the poor food in the road-houses.

Tonight we would sleep in our own beds. Our friends in Fairbanks, we discovered later, were worried that we might never return. The temperature continued to fall that Sunday morning, but the ice fog lifted, and Daddy could see to drive.

Between Tok Junction and Delta Junction and less than 100 miles from Fairbanks, there was a natural preserve where a herd of buffalo roamed. These animals often traveled the plowed roads rather than make their own paths through the snowdrifts. Suddenly, out of nowhere, three large buffalo loped onto the highway right in front of the station wagon. Once again, we were in harm's way. Daddy realized instinctively that if he stopped the station wagon we would become a setting target.

To attempt to pass these wild animals might anger them and cause them to charge the car like the moose had charged the train near Mt. McKinley. And so, for nearly twenty miles, we drove behind the buffalo, keeping a safe distance between them and us, but always moving. No one knew how long our wild animal escort would lead us or if at any moment the buffalo might turn and charge the car. All five of us were tense.

After nearly an hour, something along side the road attracted the animals, and they loped off the highway just as they had entered it. It was as if the buffalo never even knew we were behind them. We knew, though. It was exciting to be led down the highway by wild animals, but the outcome could have been disastrous, and none of us wanted anything else catastrophic to occur so close to home. We all breathed a sigh of relief when we saw the buffalo head for the open spaces.

It seemed that the closer we got to Fairbanks and our little house, the more unreachable they became. It had been fun to travel with the animals, but we were anxious to get home and being attacked by three buffalo within hours of home wasn't in our travel plans. At last, Fairbanks was in reasonable driving proximity. It was late Sunday afternoon when the buffalo escort left us, and Daddy thought that with good luck and no more wild animals, gusts of wind, or car accidents we might make it home within just a couple more hours. We would make it home at least before church was over.

At Big Delta we headed straight for Ft. Richardson and home. It was early evening, and now we were on a mission: our little house beside the church. We would spend tonight in our own beds. That was final! We were exhausted by thousands of miles of driving over dozens of different roads and highways. We were weary of being cooped up in the station wagon days on end. The roadhouses and the highway had lost their adventure and allure. The bitter cold weather, the gusty winds, and the ice storms had worn us down. We had all had enough of the Alaskan Highway. All we all wanted was our little house.

On the last day of our incredible journey of nearly 5,000 miles, the elements still weren't through teasing and threatening us. Between Big Delta and after the buffalo incident, we drove into yet another ice storm. This storm was worse than all the others put together; and a thick fog accompanied it. Daddy's driving visibility was worse than any other day of the trip.

Like he had been doing when we drove into the ditch, Daddy was scraping the window and driving at the same time. This time, though, he was keeping an eye on the shoulder, looking for the red shoulder markers. The ice and fog were so thick that he just drove and drove until there were no more markers. Neither he nor Mama could figure out what had happened to the shoulder markers or where we were.

Suddenly, they saw a familiar sign, and they began to laugh simultaneously. The sign they saw said: *2nd Street*. We were in Fairbanks. Daddy had passed our turn on *10th Street* and were in the middle of town. The weather had had the last laugh on us. Because of the poor visibility, we had driven eight blocks past the turn to our house. Daddy turned the station wagon around, and within minutes we were in front of our little house beside the church.

We had traveled thousands and thousands of miles in the new station wagon. From the beginning of the Alaskan Highway at Dawson Creek to Fairbanks had been 1,523 miles of Arctic driving. But that wasn't the half of it. There was nearly 1,200 miles of road between Shelby, Montana and Dawson. And that wasn't the half of it either. There had been over 2,000 miles of highway between Oklahoma and Shelby, Montana. And that wasn't the half of it. In addition, there were over 2,000 miles that we had driven from Seattle down the Pacific coast and across the Southwest to Kansas City in January.

What a trip! We had experienced every climate from the Pacific Northwest to the desert Southwest to the American Midwest to the Arctic. We had experienced temperatures from 90 degrees above in Arizona to over 70 degrees below on the Alaskan Highway. We had traveled on a U.S. military plane and then had the delight of taking delivery of a brand new vehicle.

Our family had slept in dozens of different beds and eaten at countless different tables. We had seen mountains and lakes and scenery that many people never experience in an entire lifetime. We had been diverted because of a frozen flood, snowbound, rescued, buried, and rescued again. We had even had a final wild animal escort into home.

What a trip this had been. At last, we were home, and it felt wonderful to be back in my little house in my basement bedroom. After an unbelievable journey of over 6,500 miles of driving, we were back in our own little house. It had been nearly two months since we left Fairbanks in December 1949 on the paratrooper plane. We were all exhausted, but we were well and thrilled to be home in our little house.

We had traveled through some of the most rugged country in North America under some of the most dangerous and adverse circumstances. Finally, on a frigid, subzero night in February 1950, we were home. How good it felt. We had traveled through eleven states, two Canadian provinces, and one Canadian territory. Our little house in the arctic had become our home, and it felt warm and good.

Chapter 13
Alaskan Escapades

During the late 40s and the early 50s people in the United States didn't fly nearly as much as they do now. Even though flying was rare, Daddy and Mama still had several friends from the lower forty-eight who were adventuresome enough to visit us in Alaska.

Traveling was drastically different in the late 40s and early 50s than it is today. Maybe there were people somewhere who stayed in hotels, but we didn't know any of them. Daddy's work was mission work, and there certainly was not enough money in the mission budget to lodge guests in hotels. With very few exceptions, all of the people who visited us in Alaska stayed with us in our little house, and often we would have more company than the little house could possibly hold.

Most of the special district meetings were held at Daddy's church, so often entire families stayed with us. Our little house was crowded already with the five of us, and adding only two more people strained it to the limits. When a family stayed with us, we literally bulged at the seams. Regardless, it was common for families to stay with us in the little house.

Daddy and Mama had friends who were missionaries in Nome on the Bering Sea. Our life was similar to outside life, but theirs was not. They received food and supplies for the whole winter during the summer via ship on the Bering Sea. Their home was an apartment attached to the rear of the mission, and the *only* tree in Nome was in their greenhouse. These friends worked exclusively with Eskimos and Indians. Nome was five hundred miles from Fairbanks by air, and their life was unfathomable to Jason and me. At least once each year, they would get away from Nome by visiting Fairbanks. And, of course, they stayed with us—in our little house.

There were five in the their family also, but that wasn't all. They traveled with a menagerie of pet rabbits, gerbils, turtles, fish, and birds. Because our house was so tiny and the winters were so long and cold, Daddy and Mama never let us have pets while we lived in Fairbanks. Mama always loved to have company, but when you added this family of five from Nome and their menagerie of pets to our family of five, we were all quickly strained to the limit. Regardless, Daddy and Mama took them in because they understood how much they needed a break from their bleak and lonely lives in Nome.

The builders of the church next door to the parsonage had considered the guest situation when they built the new church in the mid-40s. With typical Alaskan ingenuity, they had included a guest bedroom in the basement of the church. There was a bathroom in the church basement, but it had neither a shower or a bathtub. When guests stayed at the church, they came to our house to bathe. I thought it was great fun to have someone knock at the door and ask to take a bath in our tub.

More often than not, our visitors had some connection with Daddy's mission, but whether we knew the people who were visiting or not, it was always exciting to have company. And, they were always welcome to the bathroom.

Twice Daddy invited friends from Texas to fly to Fairbanks to be a special speaker at the mission. At other times, the general church conference would send dignitaries to check on Daddy's work. Regardless, these people always stayed with us in our little one-bedroom house next door to the church no matter how important they were. Daddy and Mama gave up their bedroom for our guests, and they slept on a fold down couch in the little living room. This couch wasn't a hide-a-bed with a comfortable mattress like we have today. It folded down in the middle, and whoever slept on it always rolled toward the middle. It was okay for kids, but it was extremely uncomfortable for two adults. Mama and Daddy never complained, though.

Having people visit us made Mama and Daddy feel connected to their previous lives in the states. Our guests didn't have much privacy in Mama and Daddy's bedroom, though, since the three of us still had to go through their bedroom to get down the stairs to our basement world. It was always a great joy having company. Mama would spend a lot of time in preparation, both cooking and cleaning the house.

One family visited us twice. They were old friends of Daddy and Mama. He was a preacher with a special talent as a chalk artist. She sang special music and played the piano. I thought they were the most talented two people in the whole wide world. Daddy's friend spoke at our little church every night for two weeks, and each night his wife would sing a solo and accompany herself on the piano.

The most exciting part of each evening, however, was the artistic part. As his wife played background music on the piano, Daddy's friend stood by his artist's easel and created right before our eyes what I thought was an absolute artistic masterpiece. After he finished the drawing, he would give it to someone in the audience. It was just wonderful, and he especially liked drawing Alaska scenes. Many people would come to hear Daddy's friend preach just because they wanted one of his drawings.

For two weeks we went to these church services each evening, but during the days Daddy and Mama took their friends to experience all the sights of the Arctic. Daddy and Mama became great tour guides. Daddy would load our guests into the station wagon and head for Ester Gold Mine, or we would drive on the Steese Highway to Livengood (a gold rush ghost town) or Circle City. Sometimes, Daddy would make the trip to Circle Hot Springs. Here the water was over one hundred degrees all year round.

Our guests were always treated with a tour to the University of Alaska and its amazing territorial museum. The highlight of this visit was always the giant twelve foot tall Kodiak bear. Regardless of how many times I saw that bear, I was always mesmerized by its size and ferocious appearance. It was great fun having company because they generally visited in the summers when the weather was nice. During our Alaskan summers we did a lot of picnicking, and these picnics were always more fun when shared by one or more of Daddy and Mama's outside friends.

After his first visit, Daddy's chalk artist friend and his wife wanted to return to Alaska and bring their young son, Johnny. Jason and I were thrilled when we learned that a kid was coming to visit. This was extremely rare; in fact, it happened only this one time. We loved Daddy's friends, anyway, but having them bring their son was exciting news. Jason and I had many friends in Alaska, but a kid coming to see us from the states was almost unthinkable.

When at last the big day arrived, we drove to the airport in the woody to pick up our guests—including Johnny. Johnny was eleven years old, Jason was nine, and I was seven. What fun we had together in the twenty-four hour Alaskan summers. Each night we went to church for a couple hours, but the sun was still shining when church was over, and the three of us played and played.

One day during this visit, Daddy and Mama decided to take their friends out in the countryside on one of their many tourist excursions. Jason and Johnny pleaded to stay behind, and finally— much to their surprise—they prevailed in this request. Not only did our parents agree to let the boys stay behind, but they let me stay with them as well.

This was almost too much to believe; all three of us were excited to be left alone. After Daddy and Mama and little Sammy left with their friends, Jason, Johnny, and I walked downtown. It wasn't unsafe or out of the ordinary in those days for kids to walk to town alone. Fairbanks was small, the servicemen didn't come into town until the weekends, and almost everyone in town knew who we were anyway.

During the previous winter there had been a disastrous fire in downtown Fairbanks. In fact, it was a catastrophic fire. It started in the boiler of the local jewelry store, and before it was over, more than one full city block of downtown Fairbanks was wasted. The fire department did everything possible that was known in 1950 to extinguish the fire, but it was just too cold to put out the flames. If any air got into the fire hoses, it caused the water to freeze inside the hoses, causing them to burst. As soon as the fire hoses were rolled out across the streets, they froze solid wherever they were laid. Even after the firemen from Ladd Air Force Base came into town to lend a hand to the Fairbanks Fire Department, the fire continued to burn relentlessly. It seemed to be inextinguishable.

For nearly two weeks the business section of Fairbanks smoldered, and each day the dollar loss to local businesses rose astronomically. Nonetheless, the fire was not without its allure. While the fire burned, the temperature outside hovered at fifty degrees below zero or colder every day. Wherever water touched the fire, rather than extinguishing the blaze, it froze in place, and the fire trucks froze on the streets as well.

The downtown business section began to take on a personality of its own, but not the personality of the hustling business downtown that we knew. The destruction of the fire and the frozen water from the fire hoses created an eerie beauty. The business section of Fairbanks was eventually transformed into an Arctic cavern with icy stalactites and stalagmites forming inside buildings that once held the business core of our little metropolis.

One of the businesses destroyed during the winter fire was the local newspaper. Now that it was summer, the newspaper—like most of the downtown businesses—was rebuilding. Jason and Johnny and I had no real purpose when we headed for town that day. We were just three kids having a good time on a warm, summer afternoon. Arriving at the charred ruins of the newspaper building, we began to shuffle through the debris left by the fire.

The three of us were fascinated by the lead typeset we found buried in the ashes. Fairbanks was still very much the frontier in those days. There were no computers or even typesetting machines in Alaska in the early 50s. Each day the newspaper was handset with lead strips of individual letters. Some lead strips contained commonly used phrases or groups of words. These lead strips of letters or words were hand-assembled by the typesetters to spell out the daily news. This was called typesetting.

Jason, Johnny, and I made an amazing discovery: Hundreds of these lead strips were lying on the ground in the ashes. Without a plan, the three of us began to fill our pockets with lead until we were completely loaded down with lead typeset. Together we made a corporate decision that this lead was valuable. We didn't know what, but we would create something with the lead. The longer that lead weighed in our pockets, the more we knew we just *must* to do something with it. I'm not sure who came up with our brilliant idea, but I do know that all three of us were collectively aware that this idea was the *one*.

Jason, Johnny, and I quickly headed for home to create our masterpieces before our parents returned. Our brilliant idea was to melt the lead and pour it into my toy Jell-O molds and make paperweights which we intended to give to our parents when they returned home. All three of us agreed that this was a grand plan.

Our scheme seemed ingenious to all three of us. None of us contemplated any of the consequences of this plan other than the fact that we were going to have lovely, creative gifts for our parents. And so we began. First, we put one of Mama's larger pans on a burner of the stove and then dumped all the lead typeset into it. As the burner under the pan heated, we took turns stirring the lead. While the lead melted, I found my little toy Jell-O molds to pour the lead into when it was melted. These molds were in various shapes: one was a circular ring, one was a group of grapes, and one was conical. Together we reckoned that even if one of these paperweights didn't set up, we would still have a couple good ones left to give to our parents.

If Jason or Johnny had any thoughts of pending disaster, they didn't share them with me, and I had no thoughts of disaster of my own. Disaster was imminent, though. It never dawned on my childish mind that anything could go wrong. But it did. At seven years old, I was as naïve as I could be about chemistry. Very soon, though, I had an unexpected and extremely memorable science lesson. That afternoon in Mama's little kitchen in the Arctic, I learned one unyielding scientific fact: When lead reaches 620 degrees Fahrenheit, it explodes.

And explode it did! For several seconds all three of us noticed that the lead had formed a rolling boil. Since melting lead was a new experience to all of us, we just kept stirring. The boiling lead looked a lot like Mama's fudge to Jason and me, and we knew that when fudge gets to a rolling boil, it usually needs to boil a little bit more. Since we had experience with fudge, we continued to stir the boiling lead just like we had been taught to stir boiling fudge.

Suddenly, and without warning, lead erupted everywhere. It shot straight up into the air like a small geyser. When it hit the ceiling, lead began to rain all over Mama's stove and everywhere else in her little kitchen. When the lead hit the white enamel of the stove, it immediately hardened. We were all horror-stricken. Instantly, we very aware that we "just might" be in serious trouble when our parents returned home from their sight-seeing excursion. Miraculously, none of us was burned by the hot metal.

There was no adult in the house to give us any advice. Together we went to work and did the best we could do under the circumstances to try to clean up our mess. The first thing we did after the explosion was to pour the melted lead into my little toy Jell-O and complete our project. The lead was so hot that it nearly melted the aluminum of the little molds. When the lead hardened, it fused together in one piece with the mold, and none of that lead ever came out of those toy molds; they were ruined forever.

Frantically, we set about cleaning up our mess. I remember standing on Mama's stove and scraping hardening lead off the ceiling. The only saving factor of the entire ordeal was that the lead began to harden quickly. It was easy to chip off whatever surface it struck in the eruption. I don't know how, but we did a pretty good job of cleaning up the devastation caused by the lead eruption.

Surprisingly, our parents weren't too upset about what we had done. This was only because the three of us did such a good job of cleaning up our mess. If they had seen us earlier or the mess the lead made, all four of them would have been extremely upset. I'm sure Mama would have given both Jason and me a spanking.

As it turned out all four of our parents just laughed and thought it was a funny little stunt. What *they* didn't know undoubtedly didn't hurt *us*! Twenty-five years after the lead episode, I saw Johnny at a meeting in California. Together, we began to laugh at the memory of the erupting lead. It was an experience that none of us will ever forget—and one we never attempted again.

Not all of our escapades were potentially self-destructive. Some of them were just good, healthy "kid fun." We had no television and certainly no computers or video games. We didn't have roller blades or skateboards or scooters. And there were no organized ball teams for kids in Fairbanks in the 40s and 50s. None of us kids felt cheated by the lack of these modern conveniences and activities, though. Actually, our childhood play stretched our imaginations, and we developed creative, clever, and ingenious alternatives to amuse ourselves.

On the long summer nights of the midnight sun, we played hide-and-go-seek with a base area of over a city block. All the kids in the neighborhood got into the game, and it was tremendous fun. Sometimes Mama and Daddy would lose track of time, and we might play outside to well after 10:00 P.M. There were many other outdoor summer games we liked to play: Mother-May-I? Red Rover, kick the can, jacks, hopscotch, and Flying Dutchman.

My all-time summer favorite was roller-skating. For my seventh birthday Mama and Daddy bought me a pair of the most modern skates available. Like everything else, these came from Sears and Roebuck, and I had dreamed about them all winter. These skates had a metal sole, four wheels, and adjustments to clamp around my shoes. I felt so grown-up wearing my own roller skate key around my neck to adjust my skates. I was really coming up in the world when I got skates. We did other things in our Alaskan summers, too. We climbed trees and walked fences and thoroughly enjoyed our time outdoors.

Alaska has always been dependent on airplanes. Private planes and bush planes of all sorts are abundant. Even today there are many small villages that can only be reached by plane. Wrecked cars must be stored somewhere, and we had seen them in junkyards in Texas. Alaska had a different twist on the auto junkyard. Near our little house was one of our favorite places to play: the airplane graveyard.

The airplane graveyard was similar to a car-wrecking yard or junkyard except it was full of old worn out and crashed planes. My, how we loved to climb in and out of these planes, jump off the wings, and walk up and down the aisles. Some of these planes were small one-passenger bush planes, and some were larger commercial passenger planes like the Pan American plane we flew on in 1947.

As we played, Jason and I tried to imagine who had lived or died in the crash and what it must have been like for the people on the plane when it went down. We sat in the pilot and the copilot's seats, fiddled with twisted controls, and pretended we were flying the plane. This was great fun and stretched our imaginations more than any television show. There was no place in Texas—no zoo or kid's park anywhere—that ever compared to the airplane graveyard.

Digging was also a frequent Alaskan adventure. It could sometimes be amazingly rewarding. Great rivers of moving ice buried Alaska during the Ice Age. Because of this, it was common to find remains of mastodon and other prehistoric animals in the ground. One summer, Daddy enlarged his church and began by digging a basement for the new extension. As the workers dug, they hit something solid that they instinctively knew was not permafrost. They stopped digging with machines and began to dig by hand. Several hours later, they exposed a ten foot long mastodon tusk.

The tusk was an amazing find. Daddy and Mama kept small shards of the tusk. The bulk of it, though, they donated to the University of Alaska Museum. Each spring at the end of the school year, Mama took shards of mastodon ivory to the jeweler and had them polished. Then, she had the jeweler make a tie tack or cuff links or earrings or a brooch for gifts for our teachers.

The expansion of the church building was another amazing adventure for Jason and me. Since we arrived in 1947, Daddy's little church had grown until the small building on the corner wasn't big enough to house all the activities and worship services. The people and Daddy both wanted to add on to the building, but there was no feasible way. Daddy was always ingenious and clever, and he contrived a remarkable scheme to solve the church's space dilemma.

Our little church stood on the corner of 10th and Nobel with our house next door. The little garage stood between the church and the log cabin. Daddy's idea to solve the church's space dilemma was brilliant. First, he tore down the garage behind the church and dug a basement where it had stood. When the basement walls were poured, Daddy had the church building sawed in two from top to bottom— roof to foundation. He convinced a contractor that the back part of the building could be rolled back over the newly constructed basement. After this was done, the open sides were filled in, and our little church nearly doubled in size. Everyone in town was amazed at Daddy's brilliant idea that actually worked.

What an adventuresome childhood we enjoyed. Amusement parks, summer camps, and roller coasters are exciting, but they pale compared to the life we led in Fairbanks and the Arctic. Jason and I didn't comprehend what an unusual and spectacular childhood we had until years later. After a few months in Alaska, Texas was a fading memory, and we accepted our new life as normal.

As we grew older, we learned how unusual our lives really were compared to most kids of that time. In the 40s and 50s, kids in the states were becoming immersed in the culture of early television— westerns, situation comedies, and *Howdy Doody*. Jason and I, on the other hand, were romping on wrecked planes, exploring ghost towns, playing near gold mines, and digging up prehistoric remains. Ours was a romantic childhood that would provide us a lifetime of vivid memories that would forever far surpass television, amusement parks, and movies.

Chapter 14
A Room of My Own and a BIG Scare

By my eighth birthday in the spring of 1951, Mama and Daddy decided that I should have a room of my own. Since I was the only girl in the family and I was getting older, my parents thought that I should no longer share a room with my brothers. A room of my own sounded like a terrific idea to me, but it was absolutely impossible.

There was no way! Our little house was so tiny, and Daddy and Mama nor the mission either one had the money to add a room to it. A new room for me was impossible for everyone except Mama. Daddy was creative, but so was Mama, and once Mama set her mind on anything, she always found a creative way to get it done.

Beside our little kitchen there had always been a small lean-to shed. This shed served as our back door storm porch, and we could come into it from the cold. From the shed, we could then go through another door into the kitchen. Like the real storm porch at the front door, this lean-to kept our house warmer.

Lean-to's were quite common in the pioneer days of Alaska. They were an architectural postscript. Many houses and buildings had them, and since most of the earlier buildings were literally thrown up without much forethought or planning, these little additions were everywhere. Our lean-to—like most of the Alaska additions—had no heat and little insulation. That didn't stop Mama as she set out with great enthusiasm to turn the lean-to into my new bedroom.

Daddy wasn't much of a handyman, but Mama was. The first thing she did was to take the door between the kitchen and the lean-to completely off its hinges; there was no more door. Taking down the door was the only way I could get any heat in my new room. Mama painted the walls and covered the rough, wooden floor with a scrap of linoleum she bought at the hardware store downtown.

Once my little bed was moved upstairs from the basement to the lean-to, Mama obtained two orange wooden crates from the grocery store. These rough crates were divided in the middle by another splintery piece of wood, and when they were set on their ends, these divided crates became shelves for my clothes. Across the top of the two boxes Mama placed a board, and around the whole creation she hung what she called a skirt which gave the boxes a complete look. *Voila!* These orange crates now became my very own chest of drawers and vanity table in one.

On the treadle sewing machine Mama made curtains for the tiny window of my room that matched the skirt of the orange crate furniture. Above the orange crate vanity table she hung a shelf for me to display my toys and record player, and beside the bed on the cold floor, she placed a bath mat for added warmth. The crowning feature of the room was a curtain that Mama hung over the open doorway between my new room and the kitchen. This curtain door also matched the skirt of the orange crate furniture and the window curtain, and it allowed me some privacy.

Even though Mama removed the door between my room and the kitchen, my little room was freezing during the winters. When the lean-to was built, they had added no insulation or sawdust boxes. My lean-to bedroom was still the back door entrance to our house, and people came and went through it all the time.

No one every heard me complain, though. No girl has ever been more proud to call a room her own. I was really stepping up in the world with my own room and orange crate furniture. For nearly four years I had been sleeping in the basement in the same room with Jason and Sammy. I had grown accustomed to going to sleep each night either talking to Jason or reading. I was extremely proud of my new room, but I wasn't used to being alone or accustomed to being in a quiet room. This new arrangement took some getting used to. And, at this specific time, "alone" came at a bad time for me.

While I was adjusting to this new world above ground, some events that happened in Fairbanks filled my mind with questions and my thoughts with very real anxieties. The next few months would eventually have long lasting affects on my life for years to come. As it turned out, this was probably the very time that I needed someone to talk with each night.

Epidemics and diseases have plagued the world since the earliest recorded history, but we never thought for a minute that an epidemic could affect us in our remote part of Alaska. In the winter of 1951 an epidemic was the last thing from our minds, but it soon dominated our lives. As early as recorded Egyptian history, the world had known of the disease that is today called poliomyelitis—commonly referred to as polio. (See Appendix No. 4, p. 220). In Alaska we barely even thought about polio. Jason and I didn't understand it. When we were little kids Mama took us to the doctor in Texas for shots for measles, diphtheria, and small pox. In 1946 before we moved to Alaska there had been a polio siege in San Antonio that kept us homebound for two weeks.

Mama and Daddy already had experience with Jason and me being exposed to polio. They were even more concerned than most parents because they had already seen the effects of polio on children. Jason and I, though, were young and naïve, we trusted our parents, and we didn't know we had a worry in the world. I had the round with penicillin when I punctured my eardrum, but that was an accident. There are no shots to avoid accidents.

All the kids in Fairbanks (kindergarten through high school) went to the same school, and so all the kids in town were together every single day. In the dead of winter 1951 one of the high school boys became very sick with a fever, After a few days at home, his parents thought he was improved enough to return to school.

Thinking that he was better, the boy returned to our school. He wasn't better, though, and before the week was over, he died. The autopsy revealed that he had died of polio. That's all it took. A panic of unbelievable proportion struck the very heart of Fairbanks. Every one was concerned, but no one was more concerned than our parents. Since the young man who died had come to school with a fever, every school-aged child in Fairbanks was now exposed to the polio virus.

Panic spread through our small community with rampant speed. Since the authorities believed that every child in town had been exposed to polio, this implied that all the smaller children at home had been affected as well. In reality, anyone who had even the slightest association with a child was exposed. The cycle just continued to spiral and spin out. This was potentially a complete wipeout.

The school board had an emergency meeting. At that meeting they decided that the school should be closed. To most kids today that would be exciting news, but it was frightening to us. No one knew who would be the next victim, or if someone they loved might be struck down. All of our books were sent home with us, and our parents were told to help us with our schoolwork as much as possible. School was closed until further notice.

Our parents were advised not to take us out of our homes at all. We were quarantined within our homes until it was safe—whenever that might be. Mama was even afraid to take us on our treasured library trips. I was afraid to tell Mama about an ache or admit that I had a hurt of any kind after I heard that aching muscles were a sign of polio. My imagination played all types of tricks on me whenever I had even a slight muscle twinge. I was terrified that polio would strike me.

Our tiny little house got smaller and smaller as we waited this thing out—three weeks! For three weeks the only place Daddy and Mama took us was to church on Sunday, and then we were not permitted to play with the other children. We sat beside Mama, and when church was over, we walked the few steps back across the yard between the church and our little house and waited the quarantine out another week. My nights alone in my new room became interminable, and my imagination went wild as I lay there helpless against the possibility of this dreaded, crippling disease.

Because polio strikes the spinal column, it can spread to almost anywhere in the body, and specifically to the limbs. The most severe polio patients also had their internal organs affected by the disease. As a result, their lungs, as well as other parts of their body, became incapacitated through paralysis. Scientists developed a devise to assist patients in their breathing until the initial affects of the disease subsided.

This devise was called the iron lung. An iron lung was a dreadful looking contraption. It was a round cylinder large enough to insert a human being through. The patient who could not breathe was shoved from the end of the tube through the tube until only his or her head extended on one end and their feet on the other. Then the iron lung was electrically activated, and it did the breathing for the paralyzed patient. Many people were confined to iron lungs for weeks and even months.

When we were allowed to return to school and play with others again, I was invited to a birthday party for one of my friends. My fear of polio was crystallized at that party. As I walked inside her house for the party, beside the front door was my friend's ten-year-old sister lying in an iron lung. It was all I could do to look at her; I was so afraid. I knew enough about polio by then to know that she wasn't contagious, and Mama had taught me not to be rude.

Seeing a girl just a couple of years older than me lying there so helpless only stimulated my imagination about what it would be like to be confined to an iron lung and crippled. My fear was really heightened that day, and it remained with me until I was in high school and was able to take the new polio vaccine for myself.

The epidemic that struck Fairbanks blew a hole in the "tropic disease" theory about polio. Not only did we live in Alaska, but the epidemic had raged throughout the coldest months of the year. Surely, there had to be a way to stop this dreadful disease. The big epidemic of 1952 followed our 1951 epidemic, and during 1952 nearly 58,000 cases of polio were reported in the United States alone. That was the most cases ever reported. Just like AIDS spread like wildfire at the end of the Twentieth Century, so polio wrecked havoc on the United States in the early 1950s.

Dr. Salk and Dr. Sabin had opposite ideas about how to treat polio, but they were both accurate about their theories. In 1954 Dr. Salk was allowed to test his vaccine on children who had already had polio to see if the vaccine would raise their antibody levels. The results of this experiment were positive, and in 1954 one million children were given a series of three shots as a trial vaccine against polio. Dr. Sabin and Dr. Salk continued to work on their theories, and by 1961, the polio vaccine had nearly eliminated the disease. The polio vaccine was probably the biggest medical miracle of the entire Twentieth Century, and it did not go unnoticed by me.

What a miracle that was. Jason and I had survived the biggest scare of our childhoods. We didn't do anything different from anyone else; we were just some of the fortunate ones. Children today don't even know what polio is, but those of us who lived through the epidemics of 1951 and 1952 will never forget the fear that was struck to our hearts at just the sound of the word: *P-o-l-i-o.*

We had other things to concern us as well as polio that winter because Mama had been sick again and again. Because we were home three weeks during the worst of the epidemic, she waited until summer to take care of her own needs. When summer came, Mama went to the hospital for surgery. Jason, Sammy, and I were divided up one more time while Mama was in the hospital, but soon she returned home—much improved.

Mama had never really been the same since she lost the baby that first winter in 1948, but after her surgery, she seemed renewed and back to her youthful enthusiasm. It was great to have Mama back, and it was absolutely wonderful to have the polio epidemic behind us.

Chapter 15
The Baranof

Daddy was a restless man in his early years, and by the fall of 1951, he was feeling that it was time for us to move again even though there was no reason to leave. By that time, we had lived in Alaska four years. In the eight years before we moved to Alaska, Daddy pastored four different churches in Texas and Oklahoma. Daddy just thought it was time to "move on down the road."

In those days in Daddy's denomination, it was common for pastors to move back and forth from place to place and from town to town often. Several times during his years in Fairbanks, Daddy was invited to return to the states to pastor a church, but each of those times he declined. 1952 was different; Daddy was determined to move on, but he didn't know where.

Daddy's congregation in Fairbanks *did not* want him and Mama to leave at all. They loved our family, and under Daddy's aggressive leadership, the floundering little mission that he found when he arrived in Fairbanks in 1947 had grown to into a strong, self-sufficient church—well respected in the community.

When we arrived in 1947, the mission was so weak that financial assistance was sent monthly from the denominational headquarters just to keep the doors open. Within three months of our arrival in Fairbanks, Daddy notified the general church that he no longer needed their help, and that the church was able to operate on its own. Daddy's small flock of 50 in 1947 grew to 200 in 1951. Because Alaska's population was transient, however, Daddy probably ministered to four or five times that number. His work in Alaska was completely different from his work in Texas or Oklahoma.

Daddy was determined to leave Alaska, though, and he began to contact his general conference about moving back outside to pastor a "regular" congregation. Daddy's supervisor in Kansas City was good to him and recognized that mission work in Alaska was different from work in the states. Before we moved to Alaska, every church that Daddy accepted was a little bigger than the one before. Now, after nearly five years of work, the Fairbanks church wasn't as big as the one he had left in San Antonio in 1947. Since Daddy's supervisor understood the difference between the states and Alaska, he offered Daddy a large congregation of over 500 in Ohio. And Daddy accepted.

Daddy's flock in Fairbanks was heartbroken, and they reluctantly accepted the fact that we were really leaving. Daddy resigned effective in May 1952. When we moved to Alaska in 1947, Daddy and Mama sold or gave away the little dab of furniture they owned, and for all the years we lived in Fairbanks, we lived in a furnished parsonage. When we went to the states in 1949 and took delivery of the new Ford station wagon, Daddy also sold his Hudson. Now Daddy was planning to leave Alaska, and we had neither a car nor furniture.

In order to provide funds to buy a car and furniture of our own, Mama went to work in the fall of 1951 for the first time in my life.

She found a wonderful job with Pan American World Airways. She and Daddy saved every check she earned that year so that they could buy their own car and a house full of furniture when we moved.

She and Daddy hired a babysitter for Sammy, and Mama went to work each day. We loved this. For four years we had not been able to buy fresh fruits and vegetables. They were just too expensive. Mama's job at Pan American, gave her commissary privileges. For the first time in years, we had more fresh fruit and vegetables than we knew how to handle. At first, some of the fruit spoiled in the ice box because we weren't accustomed to having it there. But we soon grew accustomed to having this wonderful luxury of shopping at the Pan American commissary and began to gobble up the fresh fruit.

In the winter of 1951 we repeated the same car-researching process of 1949. We enthusiastically studied new car brochures. Daddy and Mama struggled to decide what style and price bracket of a car they could afford. Even though Mama had the good job at Pan Am, an entire house of furniture and a new car at the same time was a huge expense. Because of the furniture, their resources were limited as to what kind of a car they could afford.

Mama and Daddy decided to buy a 1952 Chevrolet two-door coupe. We would take delivery in Seattle like we had done in '49 with the Ford. Cars had changed a lot since '49 when Daddy bought the Ford, and they had changed even more since '47 when he bought the Hudson. The Chevy was a good car, but it was cramped in the back seat with three kids and no doors. The 1952 Chevy was never as thrilling to Jason and me as the Hudson or the Ford station wagon.

When Mama wasn't working or helping Daddy in the mission that winter, she spent most of her time sorting through our things and packing just like she did in San Antonio in 1947. This time, though, we were leaving Alaska. The first thing she packed was our reading center—the blue trunk that she purchased in San Antonio. The trunk was scratched from being shipped to Alaska five years earlier, and now it was returning to the states. That trunk eventually became battered and bent, but it always went with us wherever we moved.

When we left Fairbanks Mama discovered a unique method of packing. She purchased two old fifty gallon metal fuel oil barrels. Inside these barrels she packed all her dishes and breakables using sheets, blankets, etc. to keep them from breaking. This was a strange way to pack, but it worked for her, and these old barrels kept our things from getting damaged or wet on the steamship. This method of packing was a grand idea, and Mama used the barrels again and again over the years as Daddy moved from place to place.

Spring came all too quickly in 1952, and the closer we got to our departure date, the more difficult it became for all of us—especially for Daddy and Mama. Our teachers at school were sad to see Jason and me leave. One of Jason's teachers even came to see us off at the train when we left. In the spring of 1952, Mama and Daddy thought that we would never, ever be returning to Alaska. They sensed that Alaska was now a closed chapter in our lives.

Because of this, they wanted to do something really special that we would always remember. So, they splurged and purchased steamship tickets for us to sail on a passenger ship from Seward to Seattle. This was a huge expense for Daddy and Mama. Daddy's general church conference allowed them traveling expenses back to the states, but not enough for this lavish experience. The additional money set aside from Mama's job at Pan Am paid the balance of the steamship tickets.

Fairbanks – May 18, 1952

Daddy final service was Sunday, May 18, 1952. A month before our departure, Daddy's congregation made a final plea to convince him to reconsider leaving and remain in Fairbanks. In April they presented him with a petition signed by every single member who was in Fairbanks at the time. The petition read like this:

The following members of the Fairbanks church wish to express their deep appreciation to our pastor and his wife. The past five years have been a season of growth and blessing, due in large measure to their earnest and zealous efforts. We assure them of our love and our sincere desire that the present relationship of pastor and people may continue.

The congregation chose Dr. Fitz himself to present the petition to Daddy. Daddy told us later that when he told Dr. Fitz that he was unwavering in his decision to leave, he felt like he was delivering a direct refusal to "God Himself." It was an extremely difficult day for Daddy and Mama, but in the end Daddy's mind was made up.

Daddy followed through with his plans to leave. With many tears and sad farewells Daddy held his final service in Fairbanks on May 18, 1952. We had lived in the little house on the mission compound for nearly five years, but these years would soon be only a memory since we were leaving Fairbanks for good.

On May 19, 1952, we departed from Fairbanks on the Alaska Railroad and traveled 470 miles south to Seward on the Gulf of Alaska.

This was the same trip that Mama, Jason, Sammy, and I took to Anchorage three years earlier when I had my ear trouble, but this trip in 1952 was completely different. This time we weren't going back home to the little house. On this trip we traveled beyond Anchorage another 115 miles until we reached the end of the railroad at Seward. These miles are some of the most beautiful of the entire Alaska Railroad.

The railroad passed Portage Glacier and crossed the spur that leads to Whittier. Today, tourists still board small boats at Whittier to visit the breathtaking College Fjords. On a good day at the fjords, it's possible to witness some of the most impressive calvings any-where in the world. After the train passed Whittier, we traveled through a long tunnel, crossed the final mountainous divide, and descended to Mile Number 0—Seward—of the Alaska Railroad.

Even though all five of us were excited, there was a big part of us that was tremendously sad. We thought we were saying "Good bye" to Alaska and all our friends forever. Mama and Daddy were always very positive and optimistic about life changes. This attitude of adventure rubbed off on the three of us. When we caught our first glimpse of the vast ocean and our ship resting in the harbor, our sadness was trans-formed to eager anticipation. We were leaving Alaska and our friends, but we were also embarking on another great adventure.

In 1947, Daddy shipped the Hudson to Alaska from Seattle on the *Baranof*—the flag ship of the Alaska Steamship Lines. In 1952, our family held tickets to board the same ship for our departure from Alaska. Daddy and Mama wanted to go outside in style, and the *Baranof* was the height of Alaskan cruise ship style in 1952. Eventu-ally, the *Baranof* met its demise when it crashed with the Greek freighter, the *Triton,* by Nanaimo, British Columbia. When we trav-eled on it, though, the *Baranof* was the finest ship around.

Until the mid 1950s, the Alaska Steamship Co. was the main shipping source for the territory. It had very little competition. The wealthy Guggenheims owned the company, and for many years they held as near to a monopoly as legally possible on both passenger and cargo ships sailing from Seattle to all ports in Alaska. The Canadian Pacific Railway & Steamship Co. that sailed from Vancouver, Brit-ish Columbia was their only competition. Mama and Daddy chose the Alaska Steamship Lines for our trip because they wanted to sail outside on an American ship.

Our family's Alaska steamship tickets: Seward to Seattle - May 1952

In addition to a large cargo hold, the *Baranof* also contained several upscale passenger staterooms and all the necessary state-of-the-art accommodations for passenger occupancy. Mama and Daddy wanted our last trip outside to be the very best, because they felt this should be a trip of a lifetime. To make sure we all looked our best on the cruise outside, Mama made certain that some of her salary was spent on new clothes for each of us.

The *Baranof* was scheduled to sail on May 22, 1952. Jason and I couldn't wait, and we were at the dock early that morning. The *Baranof* was absolutely breathtaking as it loomed like a floating hotel against the fog-shrouded mountainous backdrop atop the vast, gray waters of Cook Inlet. Never before had I seen anything so beautiful. It was painted a brilliant white with smoke stacks trimmed in red. It seemed bigger than life to me anchored at the wharf and secured to the docks with huge cords of rope.

As soon as the gangplank was lowered, our family boarded the ship. The interior of the ship was more spectacular and lavish than the great white hull. The purser greeted us at the end of the gangplank. "Purser" was a word I had never heard before, but I quickly learned that the purser was responsible for all the passengers during the cruise. He wore a sparkling starched white uniform with bronze buttons, gold braiding, and stripes that showed his rank of service with the steamship lines. His head was crowned with a white seaman's hat with a bill that had the same gold braiding as his uniform. He looked absolutely stunning. Except for the captain, the purser was obviously the most important person on the ship. I was impressed.

My eyes were big and my mouth was agape at the beauty of the interior of the *Baranof*. The purser invited us into a great open lounge carpeted with lush, thick carpets and furnished with a variety of couches and overstuffed chairs provided for rest and relaxation. Along the walls were shelves of books for reading and games of all kinds to while away the long hours at sea. The walls were paneled with gorgeous, polished wood paneling. All of the stairways and railings (inside and outside) were the same polished wood. Daily, this beautiful wood was rubbed down and oiled by the sailors. If I looked hard enough, I could see my reflection in its polished surface.

The purser gave us keys and directions to our staterooms, but we did not take our own luggage there. The cabin boys handled all of the luggage. None of us we had ever experienced this kind of royal treatment—even Daddy and Mama. For the five years we lived in Fairbanks, there were a few times that Mama and Daddy walked downtown for coffee or ate at a restaurant with their friends. Rarely, had we ever eaten in a restaurant, and we had never stayed in an Alaskan hotel. The steamship world was completely opposite from our ordinary life in Fairbanks. This was to be a week of unspeakable luxury.

Jason and I couldn't stand the anticipation of waiting a moment more to see our rooms. Mama and Daddy had paid for two staterooms, and they were spectacular. Jason and Daddy stayed together in Rm. 218, and Mama, Sammy, and I were next door in Rm. 220.Each side of our stateroom had a small single bed. On the wall opposite the door there was a little dressing table with three drawers to store our things. Our stateroom had the same shiny, polished wood as the stairways and the lounge by the purser's office. Inside the stateroom door was another tiny door that opened into a little bathroom.

Everything in the stateroom was compact, and I couldn't imagine how we could fit into that small room with our luggage, too. Sammy slept on a little rollaway that the cabin steward brought each night just before bedtime. Once we unpacked our things, the cabin boy stored our luggage for the rest of the trip, and while we were eating dinner, the cabin steward folded our beds down. It was magical.

Once we inspected our stateroom, Mama and Daddy gave Jason and me permission to explore the ship. The *Baranof* was a world within itself. Jason and I climbed up and down the polished wooden staircases to all four of the decks. On the bow (front) of the ship we discovered the huge anchor rest and the captain's bridge. On the aft (back) of the ship along with more of the sailors' gear was a small deck and rail for viewing.

There was a promenade deck for passengers. "Promenading" sounded so impressive to me, and while we were on the *Baranof*, I spent a lot of time on the promenade deck. This deck was about eight feet wide and was constructed from strips of wood. The promenade deck wrapped completely around the ship, and passengers could stroll or "promenade" around and around. There was shuffleboard painted on the decks, and canvas deck chairs were available from the purser for deck relaxation. This was going to be a life of leisure.

We also discovered the dining room. Without a doubt, the dining room was the most beautiful room in the ship; in fact, I thought it was the most beautiful room I had ever seen anywhere! It covered the width of the ship from port (left) to starboard (right), and around the walls were portholes draped with luscious fabrics. The dining room held numerous tables, some round and some rectangular. At the front of the room on a small dais was the captain's table situated in such a way that it looked like the captain was indeed ruling over his small empire—*The Baranof.*

Each night the captain and one or two of his crew sat at this special table in their imposing white uniforms and joined the passengers for dinner. When the captain and his entourage sat at their special table on their raised dais in their splendid uniforms, it was as though the president of the United States or the King of England had deigned to dine with us. The dining room was resplendent with dazzling crystal chandeliers. When the ship rocked and swayed with the sea, the chandeliers gently swayed back and forth as well creating an enchanting, rhythmic effect.

Mama and Daddy had indeed outdone themselves when they purchased the tickets for the *Baranof*. At today's prices, this trip seems ridiculously cheap, but in 1952, it was quite an expense for them. The total cost for all five of us was $396.75. Mama and Daddy paid full fair; they paid half fair for Jason and me, and Sammy's ticket was just $16.50. This cost included all food and lodging and cabin services for six nights and seven days. All that were left for Mama and Daddy to pay was tips. A generous tip in 1952 for a week's service on a steamship was $5.00 per person. Today's modern cruise ships suggest at least ten times that amount. The next seven days were days of adventure and romance that I shall never forget if I live to be 100.

The Baranof's front bow insignia

Chapter 16
We Leave Alaska...
but Not for Good!

The *Baranof* functioned as a luxury liner and a cargo ship for the small coastal towns along the Alaskan shoreline. After Jason and I concluded our tour of the ship, we situated ourselves on deck and watched as cargo was loaded into the hold. Longshoremen labored on the dock loading large crates of merchandise and supplies aboard. Each crate was bound with strong wire and then hoisted precariously overhead and finally lowered into the bowels of the ship.

What fascinated me most was watching the longshoremen load cars, trucks, and heavy machinery into the ship. Each vehicle was grasped from above with large metal jaws that reached completely under the truck, car, or machine. Then, the vehicle was swung around and lowered into the ship along with the crates and other cargo.

I remembered the Hudson that had been shipped on this very same ship four and a half years earlier. In some way this memory made me feel much older and experienced when I realized how much that had happened in my short life during the last five years.

Similar to the cruise ships of today, passengers on the *Baranof* were given first class attention. There were, however, major differences between the *Baranof* and today's massive modern cruise ships. To begin with, the *Baranof* was a steamship—one of the last passenger ships of its kind. Compared in size to modern cruise ships, the *Baranof* would be a tugboat. Its total tonnage, cargo and passenger capacity, and water displacement would be minute in comparison to today's cruise and party ships.

The *Baranof* was at least twenty times smaller than most of today's cruise ships. It was not just a cruise ship, because it also carried cargo to little villages along its path. There were no glamorous shore excursions offered by the purser. There were no movies or casinos for gambling on the open seas. There was no piano bar, and there was no gift shop for purchasing souvenirs.

The ship docked at several coastal villages and towns, docking whenever it reached the town regardless of the time. Passengers were only allowed to disembark the ship in two towns. Whatever sightseeing we did was totally up to us. The trip on board was an end in itself. None of this affected us in the least in 1952 when we set sail on the *Baranof*. We were traveling on board the ultimate luxury liner offered in the Territory of Alaska, and we were ecstatic.

At last, after all the passengers and more importantly, after all the cargo was loaded, we set sail from Seward. What a thrilling time that was. As the anchor was lifted and the huge ropes that bound the ship port sides were untied, her smoke stacks began to puff, her whistle blew, and we slowly slipped out into Resurrection Bay and the Gulf of Alaska. Above the ship in the salty sea breeze fluttered the American flag just above the beautiful "eight stars of gold on a field of blue"—Alaska's flag.

The entire episode played out against the panorama of the sea and mountains. Mt. Marathon and the Harding Icefield create a breath-taking backdrop for Seward, and as we sailed away, they became smaller and smaller—at last disappearing from sight. I was capti-vated, and from the very first moment we began to sail, I knew I would be a good sailor.

Once we were out to sea, the excitement of the journey only continued to build. Our family received a seating assignment at a table of ten, and we ate at that table three meals a day for the next seven days. Three times a day, one of the cabin boys walked up and down the narrow halls on the passenger decks inviting us to the next meal by playing a little tune on a small hand held xylophone. It seemed that every minute on board the *Baranof* provided another new and exciting experience.

Dinner each night was a ritual steeped in tradition. We always dressed up for dinner, and Daddy wore a suit and tie just like he wore to church. At the door of the spectacular dining room that Jason and I had discovered on our scouting expedition, we were greeted by the Chief Waiter. He, like all the other crew of the *Baranof*, wore a starched white uniform. The Chief Waiter asked Daddy our name, checked it off his list of passengers, and then ushered us to our table. Our waiter then seated Mama and me just like we were "real ladies." Wow! I loved all this elegance.

The tables, like the stewards and waiters, were adorned in white. Each table was covered with a linen tablecloth, and each place was set with creatively folded white cloth napkins and more silverware than I had ever seen at one place in my life. Mama and Daddy had briefed us before we went to dinner about how to use all the silver. It was simple: "with each course," they said, "simply work your way from the outside in." That was an easy lesson in etiquette. At the end of the first meal before we were served dessert, there was just one piece of silver left. Mama and Daddy's lesson worked. It was important to do the right thing in such a formal atmosphere, and I didn't want to make any mistakes in etiquette.

As the steward seated us, he took the napkin and snapped it in the air before placing it in our laps. This was going to be an event to remember for a lifetime. I just knew it. Beside each napkin was a printed menu that was prepared for that particular meal alone. The dinner meals had six courses: hors d'oeuvres, soup, salad, entrée, dessert, and coffee for the adults. Each course of the meal had at least two different printed choices on the menu, and we could pick and choose anything we wanted, *and* we didn't have to eat it all.

This was a kid's delight. All three meals were served with the same elegant combination of linen and silver. It was all extremely chique and marvelous. Mama had worked all winter to help pay for this trip, and she deserved to enjoy it more than anyone else. For one whole week she didn't have to cook or clean or make beds or do any of her normal housework. We enjoyed the pampering of the *Baranof*, but Mama had earned it and deserved it.

After dinner there was entertainment in the lounge. The ship had one staff member called the cruise director who organized some exciting venues for the passengers. There was something different designed for our amusement each night. Mama was trained as a girl in what was called elocution. Basically, this meant that Mama had memorized pages and pages of stories and poems. She called these "dramatic readings," and everywhere we ever lived, Mama was asked to entertain at parties and special occasions. She had an amazing ability to recite these stories and poems.

One evening the cruise director announced that there would be a talent show given by the passengers. We persuaded Mama to recite one of her famous readings. She was a big hit, and I was proud. Another night the passengers competed in a hat making style show. Mama and Daddy didn't make a hat, but we enjoyed the evening just the same.

And so the *Baranof* continued to sail through the Gulf of Alaska and out into the open seas. This didn't bother Mama, Sammy, or me. Daddy got a bit woozy a couple times. But poor Jason! He got sick the first night and stayed sick for the entire journey. I turned out to be the good sailor that I predicted I would be, but Jason was miserable for most of the seven days and six nights.

We sailed in rough, open seas for thirty-six straight hours after we left Seward. Today cruise ships take creatively planned routes from port to port. Since the *Baranof* was a cargo ship as well as a passenger ship, there were certain ports where it was necessary to either deliver or take on cargo. We crisscrossed shipping lanes back and forth making essential connections at two villages and two towns. Regardless of where we sailed—either open seas or the Inland Passage—Jason continued to have motion sickness.

By Sunday, May 25, 1952, we had been sailing in the rough, open seas of the Gulf of Alaska for nearly three days. All the passengers on the *Baranof* were anxious to get their feet firmly on solid ground if even for a few hours—especially Jason. Sitka, the historic Russian capital of Alaska, was our first and only "touristy" stop for the entire seven days.

Nothing could have prepared me for that remarkable Sunday. I wasn't aware on Saturday night when I went to sleep in my little bunk in stateroom number 220, but the next day turned out to be one of the best and most memorable of my young life. Our family awoke that Sunday morning to an absolutely gorgeous day. The sun was rising over the sound as we caught our first glimpse of Sitka nestled between the islands and the sea like a precious jewel floating in the ocean. We learned later how special a clear day really is in Southeast Alaska. In Southeast Alaska, it rains over 250 days a year, and a day of sunshine is celebrated like a holiday.

This day was my special gift. On the port side of the ship on Baranof Island sat Sitka atop a slight hill. On the port side on Kruzof Island loomed Mt. Edgecomb. Mt. Edgecomb, (Alaska's only dormant volcano), was framed by a bright blue sky the color of a robin's egg. It was so crystal clear that morning that we could see the reflection of Mt. Edgecomb in the water around us. The entire scene was breathtaking and pristine. The crisp, cool smell of fresh pine mixed with the aromas of the sea to create an unforgettable memory. Like an aerial welcoming committee, sea gulls circled the *Baranof* and escorted us into port.

Our family stood together on the deck soaking in the vastness and beauty and sunshine of Southeast Alaska. This dazzling day was certainly worth the three rough days at sea. Longshoremen soon appeared on the dock, and we watched as they tugged and pulled and tied until at last the *Baranof* was securely anchored to the wharf. With a heave and a ho, the gangplank was swung into place, and we were liberated from the ship. What a great feeling.

We knew this port-of-call would only last a few hours, so our family set out to experience Sitka to the fullest. There were no shore tourist companies waiting to snare us or take our money. Sitka's greeting committee consisted of Native Alaskans sitting along the docks selling their beaded curios and other native arts and crafts. Fairbanks had its share of Alaskan Indians, but these natives seemed different to me. Later, I learned that there is a big cultural difference between the Interior Eskimos and Indians and the Tglinkit Indians of Southeast Alaska.

The Russian trader, Alexander Baranof, established Sitka in 1804, and until April 1900 it served as the Russian capital. Before the sale of Alaska to the United States in 1867, Sitka was the headquarters of the Russian-American Company, a fur trading business. For thirty-three years Sitka remained the United States territorial capital until the capital was moved to Juneau.

Looming on Castle Hill in front of us stood the old Russian fort. This was the very site that on October 18, 1867, the Russians lowered their flag for the last time, and the United States raised the American flag for the first time. Lowering the Russian flag that day did not go smoothly, and the locals filled us in on an interesting tidbit of Alaskan history: As the story goes, when the Russian flag was lowering, the wind whipped it around the flag pole, and it would not come down. Finally, when nothing else would work, a man shinnied up the flag pole and literally cut the Russian flag from the pole. As the pieces of the Russian flagged fluttered to the new American soil below, the wife of the Russian consulate fainted dead away.

Sitka was full of history—both Russian and American. Daddy and Jason both love history, and they wanted to experience as much of Alaska's past as possible during our few hours in Sitka. Since there were no shore excursions, we struck out together to explore this historic little town. Main Street extended straight up from the docks and culminated at St. Michael's Cathedral, the historic Russian Orthodox Church. All the stores on Main Street were closed because it was Sunday, and so very quickly we arrived at the church. Just as we reached the cathedral, regular Sunday services were beginning, and Daddy insisted that we attend.

What an experience that was. St. Michael's is a beautiful old cathedral with the traditional onion dome and unique three-pronged cross of the Russian and Greek churches. We entered the cathedral through a small entryway and passed through a door that widened into a square sanctuary. The altar stood at the front of the cathedral with hand-woven tapestries behind it. The priest wore the traditional Russian clergical vestments and read chants in Russian from a large Bible and liturgy book while he swung the censor back and forth above the altar.

A few years after that Sunday, St. Michael's burned. What a loss! The citizens of Sitka were able to rescue some of the old paintings and tapestries from the fire, and later they completely restored the cathedral. Visitors who visit St. Michael's today see a restored building, but our family can actually say that we worshipped in the *real* cathedral. I'm sure that Daddy was interested in the liturgy, but the part that fascinated me most was that everyone stood during the entire service. The women stood on the right side, and the men stood on the left. What a contrast this Sunday service was to Daddy's mission in Fairbanks.

After the church service, we spent the rest of our time in Sitka exploring. We climbed Castle Hill and saw the canon that was fired for the last time the day Alaska became U.S. territory. We saw the Pioneer Home and Sheldon Jackson College. The Pioneer Home, a retirement home for aging Alaskans, is still in operation today. We visited the historic Indian cultural museum and walked through the totem poles in the wooded park overlooking the bay. We caught a glimpse of Mt. Edgecomb Indian High School on the island across the bay. Still today, Indians and Eskimos from all over the state come to Mt. Edgecomb to be educated at this boarding school.

What a magnificent day. All too soon, in the distance we began to hear the mournful wail of the ship's whistle beckoning us back to the *Baranof.* All the passengers who disembarked had been advised to listen carefully for the whistle. When it finally blew three short blasts, it was sailing. If we weren't on board then, we would be left behind.

The first long blast of the whistle succeeded like a magnet. From all parts of Sitka, *Baranof* passengers had been exploring. Now we began to stream down the streets and hills toward the awaiting gang-plank of the *Baranof.* No one wanted to be left behind. As we approached the ship, Indians entertained us with their native dances and made their final attempts to sell us their native curios. Mama and Daddy didn't buy anything to remember our day in Sitka, but we have never forgotten it regardless.

Exactly as we had done three days earlier in Seward, we boarded the ship and watched from the deck as the sailors on board labored with the longshoremen on the docks to send the ship back out to sea. And then, we cast off. By the end of May the days were lengthening, and although it was already early evening when the *Baranof* sailed, there were several hours of sunlight left.

Back on the ship, the glory of this special day continued. Before dinner that Sunday, the captain offered a small chapel service for any passengers interested in attending. He asked Daddy to conduct the service, and like I had been proud of Mama at the talent show two days earlier, I was equally proud of Daddy.

May 25, 1952, was a special day for many reasons: the beautiful day we experienced in Sitka, the opportunity to go ashore for a few hours, and my Daddy conducting the chapel service on board the ship. The biggest reason it was such a great day, though, was that May 25, 1952, was my ninth birthday! How could any nine-year-old be so privileged to have all of these amazing adventures on her birthday?

When our family arrived in the lavish dining room for dinner, I felt more special, mature, and grown-up than ever before in my short life. My birthday presents that year were the new clothes for the trip and the trip itself. I expected nothing else. Mama and Daddy had one last gift for me, though, and that was a big surprise. At dinner that night the captain himself announced my birthday, and our waiter presented our table with a birthday cake "just for me," while all the passengers in the dining room sang *Happy Birthday* to me.

One last humorous incident happened at that dinner. When my birthday was announced, a lady at our table asked me, "Young lady, where were you born?"

"Oklahoma," I responded, thinking that was something to be proud of.

Our tablemate looked stunned when she continued. "You don't look like an 'Okie,'" she said with some shock.

This now became Mama's conversation. It was her turn to be shocked. Mama addressed the lady in her customary straightforward manner. "What exactly does an 'Okie' look like?" she inquired.

Before the speechless lady could answer, Mama pressed on. "Do my husband and I look like 'Okies'?"

Things such as prejudice and diversity were never mentioned in the 50s, but they were definitely present that night at our dinner table aboard a luxury liner in the middle of the ocean. The embarrassed lady gulped and gasped and tried to recover from her *fax paus*. But Mama would not be deterred: "Both my husband and I were born and raised in Oklahoma. He has an earned college degree and a "successful" career. I'll have you know," Mama said with all her dramatic skill, "we are proud to be 'Okies'!"

Mama wasn't happy! Not at all.

Perhaps Mama could have been more diplomatic, but maybe— just maybe—she handled the situation in the very manner it deserved. Regardless, the lady spent the rest of the trip trying to recover from her social blunder. Nothing—not even an insensitive passenger— was going to mar the memory of this day. As far as I was concerned it had been perfect. What a ninth birthday. What a day!

The *Baranof* sailed south around the tip of Baranof Island and then turned north through the Chatham Strait along the west coast of Admiralty Island. We didn't get to enjoy the beauty of this part of the trip because we sailed through the strait at night.

That night we were told that at 4:00 A.M. the *Baranof* would dock in Juneau. We would be there approximately five hours. If any passengers wished to disembark, they could do so. Jason and I begged Mama and Daddy to wake us up and take us ashore at Juneau. They agreed that one of them would take us off the ship. Today cruise ship schedules are arranged so that the ships sail into Gastineau Channel and the Juneau harbor during the day. This allows passengers to experience the majesty of Mt. Roberts, Mt. Juneau, Douglas Island, and the breathtaking beauty of Alaska's capital city in the foreground.

Juneau is the only town in Southeast Alaska that is situated on the mainland rather than on an island, and it virtually erupts from the sea. Each numbered street is one block higher up the mountain. It is hard to fathom how this city was ever constructed, but it was a boom town begun during the gold rush, and the prospectors did anything necessary to attain access to the gold. When 3:30 A.M. arrived on May 26 and the ship docked at Juneau, Jason changed his mind and chose to continue sleeping.

Daddy and Mama were always adventuresome, so they left Sammy on the ship with Jason, and the three of us disembarked the *Baranof* in Juneau at 4:00 A.M. Together we walked along the semi-dark streets of Juneau. We saw the capital building, the Greek Orthodox Church, the governor's mansion, and other territorial office buildings. The three of us thought this was a lark. As Jason and Sammy slept in their stateroom, Mama and Daddy and I stood on the deck and quietly watched Juneau wake up that morning as we slipped away, and it vanished in the distance. Little did we realize that in a very short time, we would be calling Juneau our home.

On Sunday night when we sailed from Sitka in darkness, we weren't able to witness the spectacular scenery on the west side of Admiralty Island. We didn't miss Admiralty Island entirely, how-ever. As we continued south from Juneau on Monday, the *Baranof* sailed through the Stephens Passage on the eastern side of the island between it and the mainland. What a day that was. The sky was the same beautiful blue it had been on Sunday in Sitka, and around the ship we saw wild life of all sorts and varieties—both in the water and on the banks on either side of the ship.

We saw moose and bear, beaver, deer, and salmon. As we relaxed on the promenade deck and soaked up this real life travel video, there were times that our little ship sailed so close to the banks it seemed as though we could reach out and touch tree branches that hung over the water. Salmon were jumping so high in the water around us that I thought I could lean over the deck railing and catch one with my hands. At times, the wild animals were so near the ship that it appeared like they might attack it.

After the *Baranof* left Juneau she sailed through the most beautiful part of the entire journey. We sailed south through the Gastineau Channel and into the Inland Passage of Southeast Alaska. On Tuesday the *Baranof* made two quick stops to load and unload cargo. Our first stop was a little fishing village named Wrangell. Wrangell is not a tourist stop today, but it was a stop that week for the *Baranof.*

The stop in Wrangell was a brief one, and no passengers was allowed off the ship. This was disappointing to me because I was anxious for another land adventure. As we watched from the deck, we were now familiar with the loading and unloading procedure we had seen at Seward, Sitka, and Juneau. Even though Wrangell is remote, it is well-known because John Muir (who was famous for exploring Yosemite Park and the Redwoods in California) also staged Alaskan wilderness expeditions from there.

We were disappointed when we couldn't disembark at Wrangell. In a few hours, we docked at another village named Petersburg. Petersburg is a fishing town bustling with many canneries, and it is one of the most picturesque little villages in Alaska. Situated in the heart of the Tongass National Forest, Petersburg is called Alaska's "Little Norway" because its surroundings greatly resemble Norway, and Norwegian fishermen were its early settlers. Perhaps the Norwegians chose this beautiful spot for their village because it resembled their homeland.

Our journey aboard the *Baranof* was drawing to a close. On Tuesday, May 27, 1952, we sailed past the picturesque little Canadian town of Prince Rupert. Because the *Baranof* was an American ship, it was not allowed to dock there. Quietly, we sailed by Prince Rupert never once imagining that we would ever again be near there in our lives. After we passed Prince Rupert, we sailed through the Queen Charlotte Islands and Queen Charlotte Sound.

Tuesday night while we were sleeping, the *Baranof* quietly slipped along the southern coast of Vancouver Island. Tuesday morning was our last morning aboard the *Baranof*, and we had an unusual call for breakfast. The cabin boy played his usual tune on the xylophone, but he added his own personal touch to it: "Last breakfast aboard the *Baranof*," he chanted. "Eat it and beat it!"

As we enjoyed our final breakfast of this marvelous journey, the *Baranof* made its final turn around the southern tip of Vancouver Island. We sailed into the beautiful Strait of Juan de Fuca, and passed the Olympic National Park and Port Angeles, Washington. At last, the little ship turned south into the Puget Sound and the port of Seattle.

It was winter when we flew to Alaska from Seattle in 1947, and it was winter when we passed through Seattle during Christmas of 1949. It was spring now, and Washington State was bursting with rhododendrons, trillium, camellias, irises, roses, and an abundance of wild flowers. It was beautiful, and there was a sense of finality to our Alaskan experience as we saw the skyline of Seattle emerging through the morning fog.

We didn't have a home yet, and we had no furniture, but we felt like we had come home. Nearly five years earlier, Daddy had driven the Hudson to this very dock to ship it to Alaska on the *Baranof.* Now we were exiting Alaska in 1952 at the very port through which we had entered in 1947.

One last time Daddy's friends met us at the dock, and again we arrived at a new car dealership in Seattle to take delivery of yet another new car. After the proper papers were signed, Daddy was handed the keys to our new blue, two-toned 1952 Chevrolet coupe.

1952 Chevrolet 2-door coupe

The Boeing traffic was worse it seemed than it had been in 1949 with the new Ford station wagon. It was a startling reminder of the outside life we were reentering. History repeats itself, but now we would be reversing our 1947 trip. After a visit to family in Oklahoma, and after Daddy and Mama attended another convention in Kansas City, this time we would be moving to Ohio rather than returning to Texas.

Our five years in Alaska had changed us all, even little Sammy. Daddy and Mama were confident that Alaska was a "closed chapter" in our lives. Little did any of us know as we drove away from Seattle on the evening of May 28, 1952, that our time in Fairbanks had just been the first chapter in our Alaskan adventure.

But that's another whole story.

 Appendix

NUMBER 1
How a Gold Dredge Works

Once a dredge is anchored in the water by its pivot spud (14), it slowly begins the process of separating the gold from the soil and water. The buckets (6) which are six feet in diameter form a bucket line of 84 buckets that move on a conveyor belt.

This bucketline scoops gravel and dirt up from the front of the dredge and deposits it into the washing trommel (9). It is held together by series of pulleys called a bow gentry (7). These pulleys allow the bucketline operator to raise and lower the bucketline whenever necessary. The washing trommel is a huge iron cylinder with holes along its length. It spins like a giant washing machine and allows the fine tailings (4) and small gravel to fall through the holes and into the sluice boxes. The sluice box (10) separates the fine gravel from the coarse tailings (3). (Tailings are all the debris that is spit out the back, or tail, of the dredge). Coarser tailings stay in the trommel and then fall out the back onto the coarse tailings conveyor (12).

Finally, the fine tailings from the washing trommel flow along the tail sluice and are deposited behind the dredge. This process leaves only the heavy gold remaining in the sluice boxes. When the sluice boxes are full of gold, the miners simply remove the gold and continue the process of dredging.*

*Printed with permission: Zach and Willie Via, Fairbanks North Star Borough School District, 2000.

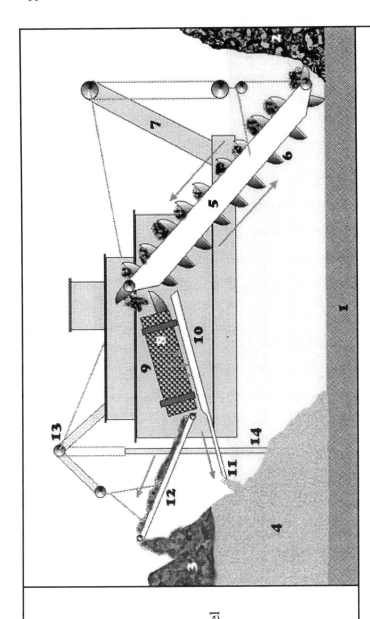

An Alaskan Gold Dredge

1 - Bedrock
2 - Gravel
3 - Coarse Tailings
4 - Fine Tailings
5 - Bucketline
6 - Digging Buckets
7 - Bow Gantry
8 - (arrows)
9 - Washing Trommel
10 - Sluice Boxes
11 - Tail Sluice
12 - Coarse Tailings Conveyor
13 - Stern Gantry
14 - Pivot Spud

NUMBER 2
The Aurora Borealis

The Aurora Borealis is a natural phenomenon of the Arctic that streaks across the northern skies near the North and South Poles in the form of arcs, clouds, and colored streaks. These arcs and colored streaks of light move and flicker quickly and appear in several colors, the most common of which is green. Although these streaks generally occur between 60 and 620 miles above the earth, auroras can still be seen with the naked eye.

These displays begin when gas particles collide in the sun's corona. They split into electrons and protons called plasma. The plasma then escapes through a hole in the sun's magnetic field in a mass eruption. It is thrown out by the rotation of the earth in an ever-widening spiral of solar wind. Electrons accelerate along the open magnetic field lines in the polar regions of the world.

Finally, the solar wind particles collide with molecules of air. Energy is transferred between them, and this lights the oxygen and nitrogen in the atmosphere like neon in tubes; thus, creating the "Northern Lights." In addition to the spectacular light displays in the polar heavens, the fast moving flow of electricity in the arcs causes them to crackle and snap. Together, the Aurora Borealis is nature's own "sound and light" show.

NUMBER 3
Chiang Kai-Shek

In 1925 a young man named Chiang Kai-Shek became the commander-in-chief of the National Republic Forces of China. For three years Chiang Kai-Shek waged war against the feuding warlords of central and northern China, bringing peace to a region of China that hadn't had peace in years. For his victory over the warlords, Chiang Kai-Shek was elected in 1928 as the chairman of the National Government of China. Even before World War II, the Japanese were attempting to conquer the whole world. In 1937, because of these warring Japanese, the Chinese were forced to declare war on the Japanese to protect their own country.

For eighteen years, Chiang Kai-Shek waged war against Japan. When Japan surrendered to President Roosevelt of the United States in August 1945 at the conclusion of World War II, they also surrendered to Chiang Kai-Shek of China. A new Chinese constitution was written, and in March of 1948, Chiang Kai-Shek became the president of the Republic of China. His victory as leader of the new China was short-lived, however.

Very soon the Chinese Communists from the north began an all-out rebellion that left China in complete chaos. In January 1949, Chiang Kai-Shek was forced to resign his position as president of China, and both he and democracy were in dreadful danger because of the threats of communism. In March 1950, Chiang fled to Taiwan where he set up the government of the Peoples Republic of China. He never returned to China as its leader.

NUMBER 4
Poliomyelitis

Polio is an acute infectious viral disease that can range from an unnoticeable mild condition to a vicious condition that can lead to paralysis or death. In the mid-1900s doctors and scientists knew that polio was easily spread through personal contact—specifically through saliva and human waste. Even though they knew what caused the disease, they did not know how to protect the public from its devastation. There was no inoculation, and when polio struck, it was a gamble whether the patient would live, die, or be paralyzed for the rest of his/her life.

Before the 1950s polio had generally stuck in relatively hot climates. The universal opinion of scientists and the public at large was that polio was a "tropical disease." In 1916 a huge epidemic of polio spread across the United States and Europe. This epidemic crippled and killed hundreds of people. President Franklin Roosevelt was the most famous American to contract polio, and the disease confined him to a wheel chair or crutches the rest of his life.

In 1952 polio struck the United States again. Before the year was over, nearly 58,000 cases of polio were reported. There was no vaccine. Two doctors, Dr. Jonas Salk and Dr. Albert Sabin, both worked feverishly to develop a vaccine to eliminate the polio. In the meantime, people waited and prayed. There was nothing else to do.

Dr. Salk and Dr. Sabin were ultimately successful with their research, and by 1961, the disease of polio had been nearly eliminated by vaccinations and oral dosages created by these two men.

Glossary

Alert: a signal given to warn of danger: *The military police blew the alert whistle to warn us that the enemy was coming.*

Amputee: one who has had a limb surgically removed: *The veteran returned from the war as an amputee.*

Bedrock: the solid rock underlying surface materials: *To build the dam safely, the engineers dug down to bedrock to lay its foundation.*

Blizzard: a long severe snowstorm with wind-driven snow and intense cold: *The winter blizzard closed all highways and stranded many travelers.*

Bonanza: something yielding a rich return: *His Dad's stock purchase turned out to be a financial bonanza.*

Boomtown: a settlement that comes to pass almost "overnight" because of something unusual: *Skagway, Alaska was a boomtown created by the discovery of gold.*

Brush: undergrowth created by vegetation in unsettled areas: *Snakes and wild animals often hide in the brush.*

Calvings: nature's phenomenon created when a chunk of an iceberg falls away from the mass: *The tourists witnessed a spectacular calving when they visited the glacier.*

Chinks: cracks or fissures created when two items are not securely connected: *The chinks in the logs had to be securely filled to keep out winter weather.*

Commissary: a shopping place provided by the military or private business that is only available to its workers: *Once a month the major stocked up on groceries at the base commissary.*

Dais: a raised platform or stage provided for royalty or important individuals: *The king sits on a dais when he greets his subjects.*

Delicacy: something pleasant to eat because it is rare: *Some people consider snails and caviar delicacies.*

Democracy: a government in which the majority of the people hold the power: *We are proud of our United States democracy.*

Denomination: a religious body with similar beliefs: *In the United States there are many different religious denominations in which to worship.*

Diversity: the condition of being different from someone else either because of race, religion, or culture.: *In the United States we attempt to respect others' diversity.*

Economy: good management and use of resources: *The economy of the United States can change from year to year.*

Etiquette: social forms prescribed by customs: *It is important to use proper etiquette when eating in a fine restaurant.*

Exemption: to officially "excuse" someone or something: *The U. S. tax laws allow people to count their family as exemptions against income tax.*

Eyesore: something that is displeasing to look at: *The run-down building was an eyesore for the community.*

Faux pas: a social blunder: *It is a faux paus to burp in public.*

Furlough: an time of rest provided for workers after a long period of work (especially overseas): *After twelve years in S. Africa, the missionary returned home for a furlough.*

Geyser: a spring that intermittently shoots up hot water and steam: *Old Faithful in Yellowstone Park is the United States' most famous geyser.*

Gingham: an inexpensive cotton-dyed fabric: *America's early settlers made a lot of clothes from gingham.*

Homestead Act of 1862: allowed a settler 1/4 section of land (160 acres). After five years the land was free and clear if the settler built a house, dug a well, plowed at least ten acres, fenced part of the land, and lived there. Another 1/4 acre could be claimed if the settler cleared ten acres of lumber: *Much of the U.S. Midwest was settled because of the free land created by the Homestead Act.*

Hors d'oeuvres: tasty foods served as appetizers: *Before the meal we enjoyed our favorite hors d'oeuvres, fried cheese.*

Incarcerated: to be imprisoned: *The lawbreaker was incarcerated for ten years.*

Inoculation: an injection of a serum or antibody to protect from disease: *The baby received her inoculations for measles, whooping cough, and polio.*

Insulation: a protection against the elements of nature: *The builders put proper insulation in the house to keep it warm.*

Jackpot: a large sum of money formed by the accumulation of bets in a lottery: *Since no one won the lottery last month, the jackpot grew measurably.*

Liturgy: rites prescribed by a denomination for public worship: *On Sunday the pastor followed the church's liturgy.*

Menagerie: a collection of wild animals: *In its purest form, a zoo is a menagerie.*

Mercury: silver-white element used in themomenters: *When the weather gets cold, the mercury drops.*

Missionaries: a person commissioned by a church to take its message to another area: *The church sent missionaries both overseas and into the inner city.*

Mukluks: Eskimo boots of sealskin or reindeer skin: *The Eskimos in the northern villages wear mukluks in the winter.*

Open Grazing: a law that allows ranchers to graze their animals wherever they roam: *Early Western farmers and ranchers quarreled because farmers felt the ranchers were ruining their farms with their open grazing.*

Outhouse: an outbuilding—usually a toilet: *Before indoor plumbing, most houses used an outhouse for a toilet.*

"Outside:" a term used by Alaskans to indicate any area other than Alaska: *To get away from the cold winter, the family went outside to California.*

Paratroopers: troops trained to jump from airplanes: *In World War II, the brave paratroopers jumped behind enemy lines.*

Parka: a hooded coat for Arctic wear: *The Eskimos wear parkas to keep them warm in the winter.*

Parsonage: a home provided by a church of its pastor: *The pastor and his family lived in the parsonage beside the church.*

Penicillin: an antibiotic produced by green mold and used against various bacteria: *The penicillin shot protected him against the germs.*

Permafrost: permanently frozen layer of Arctic earth: *The permafrost made it difficult to dig the basement during winter.*

Pioneer: one who opens up an area and prepares the way for others: *Early American pioneers broke the trails for others to follow into the West.*

Pothole: a large pit or hole in the earth's surface: *When the car hit the pothole, it broke its axle.*

Prejudice: an opinion for or against something or someone without adequate basis: *His prejudice against people of other religions was unfair.*

Prospectors: one who stakes a mineral claim: *The old prospector discovered gold on his land and claimed it as his own.*

Purser: an official on a ship who looks after the comforts of the passengers: *The purser made sure that all the passengers were comfortable as they settled onto the ship.*

Scrimshaw: articles carved on animal bone by Native Americans: *Early Eskimo scrimshaw is now considered priceless since it was not done by a machine.*

Seminary: an educational institution where one studies for the ministry: *The seminary students studied world religions.*

Silt: fine particles of earth found floating in rivers: *After the spring storm, the river looked muddy because of the silt.*

Stake: something identified for gain or loss: *He staked everything on the gold on his land.*

Temperament: a person's characteristic emotional responses: *His temperament was gentle while his brother's was more boisterous.*

Territory: a geographical area belonging to another government: *Alaska and Hawaii were the last two territories of the United States.*

Therapy: remedial treatment for bodily or mental functions: *After the car accident, the boy received therapy so he could walk again.*

Tripod: a three-legged stool or stand used to hold something up: *The photographer used a tripod to keep his camera still while he took the picture.*

Vaccine: a medical substance produced to induce immunity to a disease: *Kids in the 50s were thrilled to know that there was finally a vaccine for polio.*

Vestments: clerical robes and adornment worn by religious leaders for sacred observances: *When he conducted the mass, the priest wore his vestments.*

Warlord: a high military leader: *The Chinese warlords overran China in 1949.*

Index